Sealed for Freshness

by

DOUG STONE

SAMUEL FRENCH

FOUNDED 1830

New York   Hollywood   London   Toronto

SAMUELFRENCH.COM

IMPORTANT BILLING AND CREDIT REQUIREMENTS

All producers of *SEALED FOR FRESHNESS must* give credit to the Author of the Play in all programs distributed in connection with performances of the Play, and in all instances in which the title of the Play appears for the purposes of advertising, publicizing or otherwise exploiting the Play and /or a production. The name of the Author *must* appear on a separate line on which no other name appears, immediately following the title and *must* appear in size of type not less than fifty percent of the size of the title type.

SEALED FOR FRESHNESS was originally presented at the Pantheon Theater in New York City on April 2, 2003. It was produced by Cannon Entertainment Group, DC Productions, William Campbell and Paul Donelan. Executive producer Mike Fimiani. Directed by Doug Stone; set design by Rob Odorisio, assistant set designer Steven Capone; Costume design by Rob Bevenger, assistant costume designer Derek Lockwood; lighting by Michael Joyce; casting by Paul Donelan; production stage manager William Campbell. The cast, in order of appearance, was as follows:

BONNIE	Jill Van Note
RICHARD	Shawn Curran
JEAN	Nancy Hornback
TRACY ANN	Kate VanDevender
SINCLAIR	J.J. Van Name
DIANE	Jean Hime

The Off Broadway production of *SEALED FOR FRESHNESS* was presented at New World Stages in New York City on February 24, 2007. It was produced by Cannon Entertainment Group and Fresh Ice Productions. Executive Producer Mike Fimiani. Co-Producers William Campbell and F4 Capital Management, LLC. Associate Producer AM Productions. It was directed by Doug Stone; Set design by Rob Odorisio, assistant set designer Steven Capone; Costume design by Rob Bevenger, assistant costume designer Jeff Johnson-Doherty; Lighting by Traci Klainer, assistant lighting designer Michael Salvas; Sound by Ken Hypes, assistant sound designer Graham Johnson; Casting by Paul Donelan; General Manager Maria Di Dia, Company Manager Robert Schneider; Production Stage Manager Elizabeth Grunenwald; Costumer/Hair-Julian Arango; Propmaster-Ben Bartolone. The cast, in order of appearance was as follows:

BONNIE	Jennifer Dorr White
RICHARD	Brian Dykstra
JEAN	Nancy Hornback
TRACY ANN	Kate VanDevender
SINCLAIR	J.J. Van Name
DIANE	Patricia Dalen
Understudies	Cynthia Babak
	Shawn Curran
	Elizabeth Meadows Rouse

CAST OF CHARACTERS
(In order of appearance)

BONNIE KAPICA (pronounced "Ka-pee-ka") - 45ish. Simple housewife slightly worn by years of domestication.

RICHARD KAPICA - 45ish. Husband of Bonnie. Blue collar butch.

JEAN PAWLICKI (prounounced "Pa-lick-ee") - 35. Strong elegant presence in a small town way. The pretty sister of Sinclair.

TRACY ANN McCLAIN - 25. Naive, bubbly, girl-next-door pretty.

SINCLAIR BENEVENTE - 35. Brash, stocky, loud, been-around-the-block/extremely pregnant

DIANE WHETTLAUFER - 40ish. Plastic, upbeat saleswoman type.

THE SCENE
A typical Mid-West Tupperware party during 1968.

THE SET
A suburban blue collar living room.
Retro: Shag rugs, a liquor cart/bar,
couch, coffee/side table, chairs, etc.

WARDROBE
*All women are dressed in 1960's dresses.
Their hair and make-up should reflect the era.

*Richard should be dressed in 60's bowling garb.

AUTOR'S NOTE: Although this play is a comedy/drama, it should be played as straight forward as possible. The characters should not be cartoon-like or over-the-top. Please keep in mind that our modern sensibilities (equal rights, political correctness, etc.) have barely touched the 60's era nor the women's strictured mid-west lives

ACT I

*(BONNIE carefully ENTERS the room trying to balance a
large punch bowl — glasses hooked and clanging on the
side — full of red punch which she places on a nearby
table.)*

BONNIE. *(Yelling to the wings.)* No, Richard, it's not a
liquored-up lesbian orgy. It's a Tupperware party.

*(She then circles the living room arranging and rearrang-
ing various knick knacks for the upcoming tupperware
party.)*

RICHARD O.S. What's the difference?

BONNIE. What's the diff...*(Knows he's pressing her but-
tons, composes herself.)* I'm not even going to answer that.

*(She picks up a can of furniture polish and sprays, wipes one
of the side tables.
RICHARD ENTERS wiping his hands with a greasy rag.)*

RICHARD. Well, if you're not going to tell me what goes
on at one of these here shindigs, I can only assume that there's
subversive activity.

(BONNIE glances at a nearby plastic elephant plant, notices it is dusty, sprays one of the leaves with the furniture polish and buffs it to a sheen.)

BONNIE. Fine, if you must know, we chat about Tupperware containers that we may want to buy for the household.

RICHARD. You sit around talking about plastic containers?

BONNIE. That's what I said.

RICHARD. Plastic containers.

BONNIE. Yes, plastic containers.

RICHARD. And you don't throw in a pillow fight somewhere to liven it up?

BONNIE. No, but I'll try to fit one in between the sandwich containers and popcicle freezer pods.

RICHARD. You should.

(BONNIE sniffs the air and then sniffs RICHARD.)

BONNIE. You smell like gasoline.

RICHARD. *(Annoyed)* Really? I would think so, considering I just spilled five gallons of it on the driveway!

BONNIE. Richard, why would you do that?

RICHARD. I was bored. I didn't plan on it fer, crissakes.

(She looks out the front room window.)

BONNIE. My lord, look at that. Are those all puddles of gas?

RICHARD. Yes, those are puddles of gas! Are you not

listening?

BONNIE. Why would you do that?

RICHARD. You can thank your bone head son for mess.

BONNIE. What does he have to do with it?

RICHARD. What does he...Well "A" he didn't screw the cap on the gas can and it knocked over and spilled out all over the goddam driveway.

BONNIE. That's not his fault...you spilled it.

RICHARD. *(Ignoring her comment.)* And number "two" I wouldn't have to be using lawnmower gas had boy genius filled up after one of his joy rides. There was nothing but goddam fumes in the tank, Bon.

BONNIE. Well, he doesn't have any money.

RICHARD. Fine...then he can use the car when he gets the money.

BONNIE. Nooo, he needs the car for football practice and work.

RICHARD. Really? All I ever see him use it for is driving his cheeky girlfriend around.

(He heads to the bar and starts to make a drink.)

BONNIE. *(Chuckles)* Cheeky? Oh, her face is not fat.

RICHARD. I'm not talking about her face.

BONNIE. Richard! She has a nice figure.

RICHARD. I'm not saying it's a bad figure, I'm just saying she's got an ass on her.

BONNIE. She's not fat.

RICHARD. I'm not saying she's fat!

BONNIE. Well, if she's not fat in your opinion, what is she?

RICHARD. *(Carefully choosing his words.)* She's...she's seventeen for crying out loud.

(RICHARD rifles through his bowling ball bag.)

BONNIE. What does that mean?

RICHARD. It means she's seventeen. She's got more muscle than fat — that's all.

BONNIE. Are you comparing her muscle tone to my lack of it, hmmm?

RICHARD. No, I'm not comparing her to anyone.

BONNIE. And what are you doing looking at her butt?

(BONNIE EXITS to the kitchen.)

RICHARD. Jesus, I'm not looking at her butt!

BONNIE. *(O.S.)* You just described her butt.

RICHARD. *(Frustrated)* Awe Christ, Bon, ya can't miss it. They should put more material in those cheerleader skirts if the girls are gonna be hang'n out like that.

BONNIE. *(O.S.)* Well, you don't have to look.

RICHARD. Fine, I won't. Now drop it.

BONNIE. *(O.S.)* Besides, she's not a cheerleader, she's co-captain of the Panther's spirit squad.

RICHARD. So what the hell's that got to do with me having to fill my tank with lawnmower gas, huh?

(BONNIE RETURNS with a platter of finger sandwiches.)

BONNIE. You were young once.

RICHARD. Not that I can remember.

(RICHARD reaches for one of the sandwiches. BONNIE slaps the sandwich out of his hand sending it on to the floor.)

BONNIE. Those are not for you.

RICHARD. Look't that, you feed your hens better than you feed your husband.

(BONNIE picks it up, pulls off a hair, blows off some dust, reforms the sandwich and replaces it back to the top of the platter. RICHARD does not see her do this.)

BONNIE. Well tonight is an extra special Tupperware party. Diane Whettlaufer is coming over.

RICHARD. Ooo, I'll call Cronkite — And who the hell is Diane Waffle Laufer?

BONNIE. Diane Whettlaufer is the top Tupperware sales representative in the Midwest region.

RICHARD. Sooooo?

BONNIE. So, she's also our new neighbor. She just moved down the block into the old Reinhart place.

RICHARD. Omigod...That place is a dump. Old lady Reinhart didn't lift a finger to improve the place.

BONNIE. She was ninety-seven years old, Richard.

RICHARD. That's no excuse not ta take care of the place. My property value is going straight down the crapper as long as that shack stands. She should've hired somebody to take care of the place.

BONNIE. She couldn't.

RICHARD. You mean she wouldn't. *Cheap old bitch.* Christ, if she couldn't maintain the place after her husband died, then why the hell didn't she just move out sooner, huh?

Tell me that.

    BONNIE. She did move out — she died.

(BONNIE EXITS to get more food for the party.)

    RICHARD. *(Air let out of his rant.)* Huh...so that's why I hadn't seen her in a while. Why didn't you tell me she died?

    BONNIE. *(O.S.)* I did — six months ago. You just never listen.

    RICHARD. I listen...*(Sotto)* You just never say anything worth remembering.

(RICHARD grabs the exact sandwich that BONNIE dropped.
He hears BONNIE RETURNING and tries to quickly de-
vour the sandwich. He discovers a hair and tosses the
remainder of the sandwich in a nearby houseplant.
BONNIE RETURNS with a platter of food.)

    BONNIE. *(Beginning the line O.S.)* So anyway, Jean invited Diane over for a little Tupperware showing and to get to know the girls on the block.

    RICHARD. *(Still trying to get the bad taste out of his mouth.)* That one isn't coming, over is she?

    BONNIE. Which one?

    RICHARD. The one with the mouth of a truck driver and the breath to match.

    BONNIE. I'm guessing you mean Sinclair.

    RICHARD. If that's the name on her collar.

    BONNIE. Yes, I did invite her.

    RICHARD. Damned if I know why you put yourself through all that grief, Bon.

BONNIE. Because she's Jean's sister and our neighbor and it's the polite thing to do.

RICHARD. Polite, huh? I'd like to politely stick my foot up her dupa.

BONNIE. Richard! Besides, she's not coming anyways. She has other plans this evening.

RICHARD. *(Under his breath.)* Like grazing.

BONNIE. *(Ignoring him.)* And I wasn't going to push the issue, what with the importance of this party to Jean and all.

RICHARD. Hmmmm. Well, I don't like this Tupperware stuff one bit. It all sounds secretive.

BONNIE. You think that whenever women gather in a group it's a conspiracy against all men.

RICHARD. That's not true. I'm just saying something smells fishy here, and it's got lesbian written all over it.

BONNIE. Really, Richard, it's 1968, there is no lesbian activity. Except of course in those 8 millimeter stag films that you and your buddies show at the Moose lodge.

RICHARD. I don't know what you're talk'n about.

BONNIE. Don't deny it, Richard. I heard it from Tracy Ann McClain.

RICHARD. What does she know? She's a frigg'n idiot.

BONNIE. She knows plenty. Tracy Ann tells me Ted comes home after your meetings all frisky. Why do you think that is?

RICHARD. Jesus, Bon, Maybe it's the booze. Maybe he gets all loopy and needy on the sauce. *(Looks around for his keys.)* Where the hell are my keys?

BONNIE. But not you?

(BONNIE looks for the keys as well.)

RICHARD. Not me.

BONNIE. Okay, then what about those stains?

RICHARD. *(Caught off guard.)* What stains?

BONNIE. In your boxers.

RICHARD. What stains in my boxers?

BONNIE. You know, those deposits.

RICHARD. Deposits? I don't know what your talking about.

BONNIE. I do your laundry. I know. And they don't come out no matter how much I scrub.

RICHARD. Maybe sometimes I spill stuff on myself.

BONNIE. Really, Richard, what kinda stuff leaves a stain like that? Hmmm? Have you been drinking Shellac?

RICHARD. Alright, alright, that's enough!

BONNIE. *(Thinks a moment.)* How come you never get frisky after your meetings? Like you used to.

(BONNIE heads for the front door. She opens the door and grabs the keys out of the lock.)

RICHARD. Because we've been married for twenty years. That's why not.

(BONNIE dangles the keys in front of him.)

BONNIE. What's that supposed to mean?

(He attempts to grab them but she snatches them away.)

RICHARD. *(More irate, losing patience he grabs the keys from her.)* Jesus Christ, I gotta go. I'm late to pick up Bill and Frankie.

(Thinking the battle is over, RICHARD turns to EXIT.)

BONNIE. *(Defiant)* You look at other women.

RICHARD. *(Turning around, caught.)* What?

BONNIE. I catch you staring...all the time.

RICHARD. That's bullshit. When?

BONNIE. You stare at Richie Junior's girlfriend. *(He glances away from her.)* You watch her.

RICHARD. Bonnie, you're all whirly mad tonight.

BONNIE. You called her cheeky.

RICHARD. It's those damn skirts. Maybe I looked once.

BONNIE. She gets out of the car, you stare at her legs. She bends over — you stare. She giggles you turn to mush...

RICHARD. What?

BONNIE. You glare at her through the drapes.

RICHARD. *(Uncomfortable, trying to cover.)* You're out of your mind, do ya know that? You're going out of your frigg'n mind.

BONNIE. I see you. You think I don't. A woman knows when a man is looking... And you're looking.

RICHARD. This conversation is over.

BONNIE. It's over 'cause I'm right.

RICHARD. It's over 'cause you're insane and I'm not going to battle wits with an insane woman.

BONNIE. Insane? Am I imagining the fact that you don't look at me like you look at them?

RICHARD. I look at you.

BONNIE. The same way you look at them? Do you watch me get out of the car?

RICHARD. I have.

BONNIE. Do you see me bend over, huh? Huh? *(No response.)* Do you watch me undress for bed? *(No response.)* Is there a single stitch of desire left for me?

RICHARD. I have to go.

BONNIE. Answer the question first.

RICHARD. You're my wife, okay.

BONNIE. You say wife like I'm an inanimate object.

RICHARD. You're not an inanimate object. You talk.

(He hustles to leave.)

BONNIE. Then what am I, Richard, huh? Am I-I just a wife, Huh? Or...or...am I an object of your desire? *(Puffs up defiantly.)* Am I Cheeky?

RICHARD. Jesus Christ, you've cracked.

(Like a caged animal, RICHARD tries to leave. BONNIE continues to block his path with her questions.)

BONNIE. Why don't you touch me anymore?

RICHARD. I'm leaving.

BONNIE. Why don't you make love to me anymore?

RICHARD. Jesus, I'm tired, okay? I work my ass off 60 hours a week.

BONNIE. Not good enough.

RICHARD. Well that's all you're gonna to get.

BONNIE. Then I've gotten nothing.

RICHARD. *(Explodes)* Can you just shut up already! Huh?

BONNIE. *(Calmly)* There's got to be a reason.

RICHARD. You want to know a reason?!

BONNIE. Yes.

RICHARD. Fine...You want a reason. *(Pause)* I guess it's because...because...because, you're no longer you.

(BONNIE moves in front of him to block his attempts to EXIT.)

BONNIE. What does that mean, Richard? I'm no longer me?

RICHARD. You're not the same woman I married.

BONNIE. *(Stunned)* What does that mean?

RICHARD. I gotta go.

BONNIE. *(Quieter)* Richard, I'm still the same woman that you said your vows to twenty years ago!

(He turns and rushes to leave.)

BONNIE. *(Yelling)* Richard!

(RICHARD stops abruptly but doesn't turn around.)

BONNIE. *(Cont'd softly.)* I'm still the same woman, aren't I?

RICHARD. Yes, Bonnie...yes, you're the same woman I married twenty years ago...you just don't look like her anymore.

(RICHARD leaves. BONNIE stands motionless and dazed by his comment. She looks around as though it's the first time she's seen her surroundings. She walks aimlessly around the room.)

JEAN. *(Calling from O.S.)* Yoo-hoo...Hello? Anyone home? Bonnie, honey?

(JEAN and TRACY ANN ENTER carrying bags various covered dishes of food. BONNIE turns away and studies herself in the mirror.)

JEAN. *(CONT'D)* There you are.

TRACY ANN. Hi Bonnie.

JEAN. We saw Richard leaving. So we snuck in the side door.

TRACY ANN. He didn't look too happy.

JEAN. Which is not unusual.

TRACY ANN. I said hel-lo, and he didn't even look up. You'd figure he'd be happier on his Moose Lodge bowling night. *(Seductively singing it.)* I know my Ted is.

JEAN. By the way, we had to bring along a surprise guest.

BONNIE. Who?

TRACY ANN. *(Singing it.)* Your favorite.

BONNIE. Noooo.

JEAN. *(Nodding her head.)* Yes, my charming sister.

SINCLAIR. *(From O.S.)* Godammitt, Jean!...

BONNIE. *(Panicked)* B-but she cancelled.

(SINCLAIR wobbles onto and slowly walks across the stage carrying a jello mold. She is a massive eight months pregnant.)

SINCLAIR. Look at me, I gotta ten-pounder under the hood and you broads are doing wind sprints up the foot path.

JEAN. You have to keep up, Sinclair. We can't be delayed by the likes of a floundering sea cow.

SINCLAIR. Hi, Bonnie.

BONNIE. Hello, Sinclair.

SINCLAIR. *(She thrusts the jello mold into BONNIE'S hands.)* I brought a jello mold.

BONNIE. *(Looks at it, turns it over.)* There's no jello in the mold.

SINCLAIR. Yea, I didn't have time to make any. *(To JEAN who continues to ignore her.)* Hey, you left me out there to navigate those goddam gas puddles on my own.

JEAN. Oops.

TRACY ANN. I had to tip tow around the puddles. Luckily I took ballet at the YWCA.

JEAN. Yes, Bonnie, what's with all the gasoline?

BONNIE. Richard spilled gas all over the driveway.

SINCLAIR. I haven't seen my feet in four months and she *(Indicating JEAN.)* leaves me out there to navigate the La Brea freakin' Tar pits.

JEAN. I was hoping the Woolly Mammoth would fall in and become extinct.

(TRACY ANN laughs quietly.)

SINCLAIR. Woolly Mammoth? Why you ungrateful rat, I ought'a drop my water right here just to spite you.

JEAN. *(Unaffected)* Go right ahead, drop away, it's not my carpet.

SINCLAIR. Swear I'll do it.

(She positions herself over the throw rug.)

TRACY ANN. *(Worried, to JEAN.)* She's kidding, right?

JEAN. *(Unaffected by SINCLAIR'S behavior.)* Bonnie, is it alright if Sinclair drops her water on your new shag carpet?

(BONNIE doesn't turn to answer. SINCLAIR begins to hike up her dress and squat.)

TRACY ANN. *(To SINCLAIR.)* You're kidding, right?

SINCLAIR. Nope. And it's my fifth kid, so ya know the express aisle is wide open *(Indicates between her legs.)* no waiting. *(She pretends to push.)*

JEAN. No waiting's right. Heck, you could pass a turkey through that gully *(Points to SINCLAIR'S crotch.)* without touching the sides.

TRACY ANN. *(Repulsed)* Oh-my-god. Jean, Stop her!

SINCLAIR. *(Pushing harder.)* Ooohhh Boy!

JEAN. *(Casually)* Bonnie, she looks serious over here.

TRACY ANN. Sinclair, close those legs, you're scaring me!

JEAN. Now you know how her gynecologist feels.

SINCLAIR. Someone better get a dust pan and a mop.

JEAN. Bonnie there goes your favorite shag carpet.

(BONNIE doesn't turn around.)

BONNIE. Sure, Jean, whatever.

SINCLAIR. I'm crowning, girls!

TRACY ANN. I'm going to throw up!

(JEAN touches BONNIE'S shoulder and BONNIE finally turns around. SINCLAIR gives up on the charade and immediately stands up.)

SINCLAIR. Alright, Alright, Alright, keep your lunch down. I'm just kidding.

TRACY ANN. You're insane. Did you know that? Insane!

SINCLAIR. *(Laughs)* I'm pregnant, I'm allowed to be insane. You're damn lucky I stopped *(Plops down in the chair.)* I can dilate on command.

(Shes reaches into her purse grabs some gum and shoves a piece in her mouth.)

TRACY ANN. *(Defiantly)* You almost made me throw up my Swanson's Salsbury steak dinner.

SINCLAIR. Maybe that's a good thing.

JEAN. *(Goes to BONNIE.)* Bon are you okay?

BONNIE. *(Snaps out of it.)* Oh, yes, I'm fine. I guess I just got a little spacey there.

JEAN. A little spacey? You're walking in the clouds, honey. What's wrong? Did you get into a fight with Richard?

SINCLAIR. *(Shoves more gum in her mouth.)* Bet she did.

BONNIE. *(Changes the subject.)* Can I get you girls something to drink?

(BONNIE steps over to the liquor cart - bar and begins to make herself a stiff scotch.)

SINCLAIR. I thought you'd never ask...extra dry martini — vodka — three olives — stirred.

BONNIE. I thought you drank gin.

SINCLAIR. Eh, I had to lay off gin. It started to make my vagina dry up.

TRACY ANN. What?!

SINCLAIR. Yep, bone dry, eh...something about the juniper berries affects the squirty glands. Doctor sez it's not good to have a dry vagina when delivering a baby — sticks to the sides.

JEAN. *(Puts her hand over her face.)* Oh Lord.

TRACY ANN. *(Gags, covers her mouth and clutches her stomach.)* I just tasted Salsbury steak again.

SINCLAIR. So bring on the juice, Bon.

JEAN. No, no, no...I hate to put the brakes on your alcoholism...BUT as your Tupperware block sales representative, I must enforce the rules. There is to be no drinking at a Tupperware party. Especially if the top regional sales representative is coming over.

SINCLAIR. How much fun is this going to be?

JEAN. Kitchenware is not supposed to be fun, it's supposed to be versatile and long lasting.

SINCLAIR. I'd be more interested if I was looking through the haze of a martini.

JEAN. Well you'll have to curb your crutch for just one night. I need to make a good impression on Diane Whettlaufer.

TRACY ANN. What makes Diane Whettlaufer so important?

JEAN. Oh, Diane Whettlaufer she is a pioneer in the technique of Tupperware sales. Why, she turned the sale of kitchen storage containers into a true career. *(Welling up with pride — JEAN rises crosses to TRACY ANN.)* A career that a woman can build upon, while creating a foundation of respect and pride in the eyes of not only women...no...but all-mankind-alike...

(She stands stiff and proud while reaching off into the distance.)

TRACY ANN. *(Elated by the speech she reaches off into the distance as well.)* Ohhhhh! I love it!

SINCLAIR. *(Breaking the moment.)* She sells plastic containers.

JEAN. *(Brought back to reality, she clears her throat.)* Everyone needs kitchen storage containers, Sinclair. Some people just don't know it and they need to be told they need them by someone who knows how to tell them they need them.

(SINCLAIR shifts uneasily in the chair. Note: it's important that SINCLAIR is a bulging, uncomfortable pregnant — grunts and wheezes are not uncommon during even the least amount of movement.)

TRACY ANN. And Diane Whettlaufer is that someone to tell me that I need something that I didn't want before?

JEAN. Precisely.

(The doorbell rings. No one moves to answer it. All look at bonnie who is now busy guzzling her scotch. A second doorbell ring finally snaps her out of the daze.)

BONNIE. *(Putting her glass down.)* I'll get it.
SINCLAIR. *(Loud whisper.)* I still need a drink.

*(SINCLAIR now sits with her legs spread wide open. This next
section is done in a loud whisper, stage whisper which
builds gradually in volume.)*

JEAN. Drink some punch.

SINCLAIR. I hate punch.

JEAN. The punch is fine.

SINCLAIR. It has too much sugar.

TRACY ANN. Too much sugar will give you diabetes.

SINCLAIR. That's right...Ya see that? I'll get diabetes
and they'll have to chop my legs off.

JEAN. *(Raises her fist to SINCLAIR.)* You'll be getting
some type of punch in a minute, ya beast. I swear to God I'll
beat the living crap outta ya...

DIANE. *(O.S.)* No, the bags aren't that heavy...

BONNIE. *(O.S.)* Let me help...

*(JEAN regains composure at the sound of DIANE and BON-
NIE approaching. She spots sinclair's open legs.)*

JEAN. *(Whisper, yell.)* Close your legs.
SINCLAIR. I need the air.

*(JEAN shoots her another dirty look. SINCLAIR closes her
legs. DIANE ENTERS carrying handfuls of bags.)*

DIANE. I don't know if you know it , but there's gasoline
all over your driveway.

BONNIE. Yes, My husband had a mishap with a gasoline can earlier.

DIANE. For a moment there I thought I pulled into a Texaco Station...Ding, Ding, fill'er up. Just kidding.

JEAN. *(Singing her name.)* Diane, dear!

(Without thinking DIANE hands the last of the bags to BON-NIE who is now saddled with all of them.)

DIANE. *(Singing back.)* Jean, darling!

(They give each other a superficial hug and kiss on the cheek as BONNIE arranges the bags in the living room.)

JEAN. How long has it been?

DIANE. At least 2 years.

JEAN. At least.

DIANE. The Phoenix spring jamboree, right?

JEAN. The theme was "Storage for a New Generation."

DIANE. *(Almost cheerleader like.)* Sealed for Fresh-ness...

JEAN. *(She mirrors DIANE'S hand gestures.)* Storage for fun...

DIANE. Makes Tupperware families...

JEAN. All number one...

DIANE. You remember.

JEAN. I do. That was fun!

(They both giggle. BONNIE arranges the bags in the living room.)

JEAN. *(Cont'd)* Now, let me introduce you to the ladies. You've already met your hostess Bonnie Kapica.

(BONNIE bends her back like she strained it.)

BONNIE. *(Winded)* We've met.

(TRACY ANN stands nervously in anticipation of meeting the great DIANE.)

JEAN. And this is Tracy Ann McClain.
TRACY ANN. *(Shaking DIANE'S hand vigorously.)* I've heard so much about you.
DIANE. *(Trying to pull away from the grip.)* Don't believe a word of it...*(Leans in, whispers.)* Unless it makes me sound thinner and younger.

(DIANE JEAN and TRACY ANN giggle. BONNIE forces a smile.
SINCLAIR clears her throat for attention. The girls don't hear her. She clears her throats even louder like she's clearing a phlegm ball. This silences the hens.)

SINCLAIR. *(Casually)* Hairball.
JEAN. *(Like a bad taste in her mouth.)* Excuse that... *(Clears her throat.)* that is my sister, Sinclair.
DIANE. I didn't know you had a sister.
SINCLAIR. We're twins.
DIANE. *(Off guard.)* Twins? Huh.

(Confused, DIANE gives them both the twice over.)

JEAN. *(Uncomfortable laugh.)* Twins — Such a kidder...
(Indicates that she's obviously the pretty one of the two.) I
mean look't at us.

SINCLAIR. I'm the pretty one.

*(Always the salesman, DIANE moves towards SINCLAIR with
her hand out to shake.)*

DIANE. Well, uh, it's a pleasure to meet you.

SINCLAIR. I'd get up to curtsy, but I've got a fifty pound
fetus anchoring down my cooty-coo.

DIANE. *(Really looks at her.)* Oh my, yes you do, indeed.
Th-that does look rather...heavy. How far along are you?

SINCLAIR. Four kids too many.

TRACY ANN. Sinclair is eight months along.

DIANE. When's your due date?

SINCLAIR. Any minute, honey.

*(She bends down to look under her housedress.
JEAN reaches down to stop her from lifting her housedress.)*

JEAN. *(Bursting out with an uncomfortable laugh.)*
Noooo, she's just joking with you. She's due in three weeks.
(JEAN gently leads DIANE away from SINCLAIR.) Here,
why don't you have a seat over on the comfy couch and you
can show us the new fall line.

(JEAN raises her fist to SINCLAIR behind DIANE'S back)

SINCLAIR. Boy, there are some violent people in the
world, huh, Jean?

JEAN. What's even worse are the filthy animals that incite that violence.

(SINCLAIR bites the air towards JEAN.)

DIANE. *(Unaware of their spat.)* Yes, I know what you're all talking about, those poor boys in Vietnam — all that violence. War is such an inconvenience. Do any of you have boys in the service?

JEAN. No, but close, Bonnie has a son who's seventeen.

DIANE. You have a seventeen-year-old? Is that so, Bonnie? Why you don't look old enough to have a son who's seventeen.

BONNIE. *(Flattered, touches her hair.)* Really?

DIANE. Really.

SINCLAIR. *(Starts laughing.)* Oh Pu-lease...she looks like she could have two seventeen-year-olds stacked on top of each other.

BONNIE. Hush up, Sinclair!

SINCLAIR. Oh, the host finally speaks.

BONNIE. I have a lot on my mind.

TRACY ANN. *(To DIANE attempting to avoid conflict.)* Would you like something to drink?

JEAN. Yes, have something to drink.

DIANE. Well, that punch looks tasty.

JEAN. That's right, have some punch.

TRACY ANN. I like punch.

SINCLAIR. *(Imitating her.)* I like punch.

(TRACY ANN shoots her an evil look while pouring a glass for all the women. She passes out the punch throughout the following story.)

TRACY ANN. Ya know, every Sunday my Aunt Jenny would bring two big jugs of punch to my Sunday school class. Now I don't know what she put in that punch, but one day between that punch and the rice crispy squares little Bobby Bencroft got all wacky-doo. He took one of the big crucifix statues and was flying Jesus on a cross like an airplane. He was wild-eyed and foaming at the mouth and screaming, " watch out below you sinners, cause the squadron of Christ is coming to drop a sinner bomb on your house."

DIANE. Oh my.

SINCLAIR. I'm sure there's more.

TRACY ANN. Yes. Well, after that, Pastor Paul didn't allow Aunt Jenny to bring anymore punch around. *(Pauses)* We never did see Bobby after that day. I think he ended up in one of those military schools for the deranged. Last I heard he was a minister and part time crop duster in Baton Rouge.

SINCLAIR. *(Feigning excitement.)* Wow, you should write that story down and publish it.

TRACY ANN. Do you think? Really?

SINCLAIR. No.

DIANE. Yum, that's good — *(The sweetness makes her cough, choke.)* sweet.

BONNIE. Too much? I did what the packet said — two cups of sugar per packet.

JEAN. Why, two cups of sugar is not that much at all.

BONNIE. That's what the packet said. I'll show you.

(BONNIE heads for the kitchen. JEAN gets up to stop her.)

JEAN. No, it's okay, Bon...

SINCLAIR. *(Leaning to DIANE.)* Hey, Laufer, do you have diabetes?

(JEAN stops dead in her tracks, groans and slowly turns around.)

DIANE. *(Taken off guard.)* I'm sorry?

SINCLAIR. See, Jean here was trying to get me to drink the punch but I was worried about getting diabetes and getting my legs chopped off.

DIANE. Oh?

JEAN. Sinclair, Diane doesn't want to hear this.

DIANE. I'm not really sure what I'm hearing here.

SINCLAIR. But Jean...get this, Jean, being the good samaritan and sweet sister that she is, offered to carry me around legless and all. Ain't that right, Jean?

JEAN. No.

SINCLAIR. No? So you'd just let me flounder about in the fruit isle of a supermarket?

SINCLAIR. while folks thumped melons and squeezed nectarines all around me. Till one polite old lady who pitied my situation would kindly ask, "How did it happen dear?" And I'd say, "Why I lost my legs at a Tupperware party, ma'am." And she'd say, "What a shame, I had an Aunt who lost her legs the very same way, here's a quarter to go towards your prosthetics."

(BONNIE RETURNS reading the back of a kool-aid packet.)

TRACY ANN. That's so sad. I mean how much of a fake leg could you buy with a quarter?

SINCLAIR. So, would you carry me around the super-market, Jean?

(All turn to look at JEAN'S response.)

JEAN. *(Uncomfortable laugh/chiseling it out of her mouth.)* well...of course I would carry you around the super-market, *(Gritting her teeth at SINCLAIR.)* O-kay?

TRACY ANN. That's real sweet of you, Jean.

SINCLAIR. Sweet like that punch you're drinking. Which leads me to my next question, Mrs. Whettlaufer...

DIANE. Please, call me Diane.

SINCLAIR. Fine. Diane, how come we can't have drinks at this Tupperware party?

DIANE. *(Lifts her glass.)* We have drinks.

TRACY ANN. This stuff's like liquid candy, huh? I like it.

JEAN. No one needs to be drinking, *(Without turning to SINCLAIR.)* especially Sinclair.

BONNIE. You know how she gets.

SINCLAIR. No, tell me. How do I get?

BONNIE. Well, you get...

TRACY ANN. Angry.

BONNIE. That's it — angry.

SINCLAIR. Well, I don't see it.

TRACY ANN. Then you need glasses.

SINCLAIR. Pipe down, Idaho.

DIANE. We usually don't drink at these events, Sinclair.

JEAN. No, we don't.

SINCLAIR. Is that a Tupper rule?

DIANE. No, I just think alcohol will impair our ability to...to...

SINCLAIR. Would it impair our ability to fly jets and helicopters and drive big dump trucks full'a dirt, huh?

DIANE. Well yes, of course, surely it would impair...

SINCLAIR. Swell, we're on the same page. Question... *(Leans over to DIANE.)* Do ya think...we could safely buy plastic containers on alcohol then?

DIANE. I see where you're going with this. I'm just saying that it's usually not done and it may impair our ability to have a good party.

SINCLAIR. O-kay, but don't say I didn't warn you of the consequences of drinking this sugary toilet water...no offense, Bonnie...

BONNIE. *(Defensive)* The directions said two cups right on the back of the packet. *(She holds out the Kool-Aid packet to JEAN.)* See? Right here it says...

JEAN. *(Stopping BONNIE.)* We believe you, dear.

SINCLAIR. Okay then, we live in a democracy, we'll vote. All in favor of getting hit by the booze bus raise their hand.

(SINCLAIR raises her hand, BONNIE quickly follows.)

BONNIE, Well, I don't want to be responsible for gett'n your...you know — legs *(Indicates a chopping motion at the knee.)* off.

TRACY ANN. *(Raising her hand, looking apologetically at JEAN.)* My legs are my best feature.

DIANE. Well, I don't know about this.

SINCLAIR. *(Leaning to DIANE.)* Laufer...Hey, Laufer *(Finally get's DIANE'S attention.)*...I think you'd make a ton of sales, if my — *(Winks at her about the others.)* Our judgement was impaired by alcohol. *(Pointing at her stomach.)* I mean look at the piss poor judgement I made on a bottle of Blue Nun.

(DIANE immediately raises her hand. JEAN looks around the room, then raises her hand.)

BONNIE. Jean?

JEAN. *(Giving in.)* Well I don't want to get a hernia carrying you all around.

(The ladies laugh.)

SINCLAIR. That's the spirit. All aboard the booze bus.

(BONNIE heads over to the liquor cart and begins making drinks.)

BONNIE. O-kay, who wants what?

SINCLAIR. I said it once, I'll say it again, extra dry martini...

BONNIE. Gin...*(Catches herself.)* no, vodka.

SINCLAIR. That's right.

BONNIE. Don't want anything drying up, do we?

TRACY ANN. Nope...sticks to the sides.

BONNIE. Jean?

JEAN. Manhattan.

DIANE. I'll have a Manhattan as well.

BONNIE. Tracy Ann?

TRACY ANN. Well I don't usually drink. So maybe something sweet. How about those Manhattan drinkees? Are they sweet?

DIANE. They have sweet vermouth in them.

SINCLAIR. And a cherry.

TRACY ANN. I like cherries. I'll try one.

BONNIE. Oh, this should be interesting.

TRACY ANN. You know, Jean, about what you were saying earlier.

JEAN. What was that?

TRACY ANN. About the hernias. You definitely don't want to get a hernia.

JEAN. I'm not worrying too much about it.

TRACY ANN. Well you should....See, back in the summer of '59, my Uncle Rodney got a hernia moving the engine block of a '55 Chevy. He was a big man so he was always attempting to move big objects on his own. Well, the pressure and strain built up so much in his gut that one of his, uh... uh...

JEAN. His what, dear?

TRACY ANN. You know, his...things.

(She points down near her crotch.)

JEAN. Things?

SINCLAIR. His balls.

TRACY ANN. Yes, one of those actually tore clean through his...his...loose skin...

SINCLAIR. Oh, sweet Jesus!

BONNIE. His loose skin?

JEAN. His scrotum.

TRACY ANN. Yes, that. One of his things tore through that and rolled down his pant leg into his boot. *(Pause)* My Aunt Jenny heard the pop clear into the sewing room while she was vacuuming. She said it sounded like a starter pistol going off, but louder.

DIANE. She heard the...pop...while vacuuming?

TRACY ANN. *(Making a popping sound.)* Pretty loud, huh? Anyway the doctor said it was lucky his thing only fell into his boot on account'a it's tough to get driveway gravel off 'em.

JEAN. Does the doctor have to get gravel off a lot of... orphaned testicles where your from?

TRACY ANN. Actually, it's quite common in Steamboat Rock, Iowa.

DIANE & JEAN. Really?

TRACY ANN. Yes...the men are always trying to lift thresher parts and auger attachments and railroad ties. They're always straining something or retching something or popping something out of somewhere. And after one of those accidents, the menfolk really seem to form a kinship with the other neutered farm animals on account'a they're missin' their...

JEAN. *(Interrupts with a loud uncomfortable laugh.)* We get it, dear.

DIANE. *(Dumfounded)* Huh.

TRACY ANN. After the operation Uncle Rodney had to wear a truss all summer.

BONNIE. I didn't know you can re-attach a testicle.

TRACY ANN. Oh they never did. They didn't find it until they got to the emergency room and removed his boot and by then it was in no shape to be re-attached.

DIANE. So he never got it back?

TRACY ANN. Oh he has it he keeps it in a jelly jar in the cellar next to the cling peaches.

SINCLAIR. *(Leans to DIANE.)* So, Laufer, how's it feel to meet insanity head on?

(BONNIE hands sinclair her martini.
SINCLAIR takes out the gum she's been chewing and puts it
on the corner of the glass.)

BONNIE. Stirred, just the way you like it.
SINCLAIR. Mother's milk.

(Rapidly smacks her lips.)

TRACY ANN. Sinclair, is that really such a good idea?
SINCLAIR. I don't like shaken martini's, sweetcheeks.
TRACY ANN. No, I mean with the baby and all.

SINCLAIR. I'm sure if the baby was here he'd prefer stirred martini's as well.

TRACY ANN. No, I mean I was reading an article in Life magazine recently, and the article said that drinking alcohol may have some adverse reactions on the baby.

DIANE. I read that article.

SINCLAIR. Hey, having a baby is an adverse reaction on the mother. I drink to deal with having babies. Besides, I was hammered during the pregnancy of my last four kids — they turned out just fine.

JEAN. What about Frankie Junior? Tell me he doesn't have a loose screw.

SINCLAIR. I beg your pardon.

JEAN. Beg all you want. The bottom line is your kid's a nutbag.

BONNIE. That's a terrible thing to say, Jean.

JEAN. Have you met Frankie Junior? *(Turns to DIANE.)* The kid eats grass.

DIANE. Lots of children eat grass.

JEAN. True, but directly from the lawnmower bag?

SINCLAIR. Hey, the kid likes his roughage. What can I say?

TRACY ANN. It could be that the alcohol has effected his mental growth.

SINCLAIR. Drop it, science Sally! Listen, scientists have split atoms and built Rockets and invented saccharin, right? Hell, I think by now they'd know if booze was bad for babies.

BONNIE. I'm sure they'd know alright. Rockets have to be more complex than a fetus.

DIANE. I'll bet you're right.

(SINCLAIR picks up her purse and starts to sift through it. She pulls out a pack of cigarettes.)

SINCLAIR. And I'm sure by now those scientists would tell us if anything was bad for us.

(She puts the cigarette in her mouth.)

BONNIE. Sinclair, you know there's no smoking in my

house. If you want to smoke you can go outside.

JEAN. Please do.

SINCLAIR. Fer the love'a...*(Takes the cigarette out of her mouth.)* you're gonna make a pregnant woman smoke outside?

BONNIE. Yes.

SINCLAIR. Fine, can't find any matches anyway...[Fascist]

BONNIE. Excuse me?!

TRACY ANN. Do you have any children, Diane?

DIANE. No. No, I don't.

TRACY ANN. Do you want children?

DIANE. Well, I did...that was before.

TRACY ANN. Before what?

JEAN. Diane might not want to discuss this, Tracy Ann.

DIANE. It's okay. I wanted children before my husband... passed on.

BONNIE. Oh, we didn't know, Diane.

TRACY ANN. Where'd he pass on to?

JEAN. *(Makes a swooping gesture towards the sky.)* He passed on, Tracy Ann.

TRACY ANN. *(Embarrassed, imitates JEAN'S gesture.)* Ohhhhh, he passed on, I see. I'm so sorry.

DIANE. It's okay, it's been a while. I hardly miss him anymore.

TRACY ANN. And you never re-married?

DIANE. Never got around to it.

SINCLAIR. And why's that?

BONNIE. Sinclair!

SINCLAIR. What? It's a legitimate question.

DIANE. I guess I just never met anyone worth marrying.

SINCLAIR. Christ, none of them are actually worth marrying.

JEAN. My husband was worth marrying.

SINCLAIR. That's 'cause he sweats money.

JEAN. No, it was because of love.

SINCLAIR. Love of money.

JEAN. *(Uncomfortable joke.)* Well it doesn't hurt.

SINCLAIR. I'll bet. Laufer, you ought'a try that. Go out and get a rich guy. I'm sure you meet plenty of men on your Tupper rounds.

DIANE. No, most are married.

SINCLAIR. Well if you can't find one on your own, steal one from someone else. Like Tracy Ann here.

TRACY ANN. *(Acts appalled a beat then nods her head in agreement as though she knows she's happy she stole him.)* Yea...well, Ted was in the process of getting a divorce!

BONNIE. Yep, he moved one out and another one in.

TRACY ANN. Ted's ex-wife was cheating on him with a traveling salesman selling Amway. Ted caught them on the sun porch.

SINCLAIR. Yea, he was giving her his sales pitch and she was swallowing every word of it.

DIANE. That's terrible.

TRACY ANN. Not really ya get used to breathing through your nose...

BONNIE. *(Quickly changing the subject.)* Sooo, Diane, how do you like living here?

DIANE. Well, the town seems nice. The people are nice. It's a nice place overall.

SINCLAIR. *(Sarcastic)* Nice, nice, nice.

DIANE. *(To BONNIE, ignoring SINCLAIR'S sarcasm.)* And how long have you lived here?

BONNIE. It's been 20 years. Richard and I bought this house a couple of weeks after we got married.

DIANE. And you've kept it up so nicely. It's very...

SINCLAIR. Lived in.

DIANE. I was going to say "homey".

BONNIE. Actually, homely would be the appropriate word.

DIANE. Nonsense, I've been inside hundreds of homes just like this one. Sure there's a scuff or a ding, here or there, but that's what makes each one so unique.

SINCLAIR. Are you sure it's not the smell of the vomit and dirty diapers?

DIANE. I suppose that's part of it...but when I walk into a home that has children, there's always a presence of family...a sense of character. *(Looks dreamily around the room.)*...in every knick knack...and photograph, all the way from the ceiling to the foundation.

BONNIE. Character is what you call it? Oh, we've got character alright. All that you see is years and years of painted over use and abuse.

DIANE. And that's what makes a home so special.

BONNIE. *(Skeptical)* That's special to you? Years of use and abuse is special? Huh.

DIANE. No, what's special is the love and care that goes into fixing it.

BONNIE. And who usually does all the fixing?

DIANE. I don't understand.

BONNIE. Who patches up the use and abuse? Who fills the holes?

TRACY ANN. My Ted does when he's not taking a nap.

DIANE. There you go, a husband patches up the holes.

BONNIE. Really? Are you sure a husband isn't the one creating all the holes in the first place? *(Pauses, catches herself.)* Excuse me a moment, I have egg rolls in the oven.

(BONNIE leaves the room.)

DIANE. Did I say something wrong?

JEAN. No, Bonnie's been a little off today.

SINCLAIR. Off the wall.

DIANE. I hope I didn't say anything wrong.

JEAN. You're fine.

SINCLAIR. Laufer, if you like the use and abuse in this house, you oughta come over to my place and see how I've been scrubbing and flushing love down the toilets for years. It'd make your heart go pit-a-pat.

JEAN. It'd make her nauseous.

SINCLAIR. Sorry, Miss six bedroom house on the hill.

JEAN. Jealousy is very unbecoming of you, Sinclair.

SINCLAIR. Jealous? *(To DIANE.)* She's got a living room that no one can go into. There's plastic on the furniture, and she rakes the shag carpet twice a week.

JEAN. *(Proudly)* Two times every week.

SINCLAIR. Christ, she's such a neat freak you can eat off the bathroom floor.

JEAN. You ought'a try cleaning once in a while.

SINCLAIR. You gotta problem with my house cleaning now?

JEAN. It's just shy of repulsive...

SINCLAIR. Why, you picky little...

JEAN. *(Quickly changing the subject.)* Speaking of homes, how do you like the Reinhart house, Diane?

DIANE. Fine, I suppose.

TRACY ANN. The Reinharts lived there forever...just the two of them. Then he died, and she lived there...all alone... right up until the day she died. It's a shame though, they never did have any children. Actually, I don't think that house ever had a child in it.

DIANE. *(Hits a nerve but tries to act composed.)* And it probably never will at the rate I'm going.

TRACY ANN. *(Realizes what she's said.)* No, no, I meant...I'm sorry, I didn't mean...It just seems so big and empty for one person.

DIANE. *(Feigning joy.)* Au contrair. Big and empty is perfect for me.

(BONNIE ENTERS with a small tray of egg rolls.)

SINCLAIR. Just in time, I need another drink. All this homey talk is making me thirsty.

TRACY ANN. *(Sips some more of her drink.)* This Manhattan is really not that sweet but it makes me all warm inside.

SINCLAIR. That's internal bleeding, cupcake.

(TRACY ANN reacts by touching her stomach. BONNIE takes their glasses and returns to the bar. DIANE follows her up.)

DIANE. Did I say something wrong, Bonnie?

BONNIE. No, of course not. I'm sorry, I just have a lot on my mind — nothing that concerns you, really.

DIANE. Are you sure?

BONNIE. *(Reassuring smile.)* Of course. Now relax — Have an egg roll.

DIANE. No...No...No I have to watch the old derriere.

BONNIE. They're La Choys.

TRACY ANN. La Choys, I love chinese people.

(SINCLAIR reaches for the egg rolls with her fingers.)

JEAN. For Pete's sake, use a toothpick.

SINCLAIR. What the hell do ya think fingers are for?

TRACY ANN. *(Unconsciously interjects.)* Pick'n stuff out of parts of your body.

JEAN. *(Uncomfortable laugh, changing the mood.)* Alright, enough with the chit chat, let's get down to the reason we're all here...the new Tupperware is in!

DIANE. Yes, of course, that's why I'm here, the new Tupperware.

TRACY ANN. I still haven't worn out the containers I bought from you last time, Jean.

JEAN. And you won't. That's because durability is their middle name.

DIANE. Don't forget freshness.

JEAN. Yes, they keep things fresh, but durability is the key.

TRACY ANN. They'll probably last forever.

SINCLAIR. Like this party.

JEAN. *(Shoots SINCLAIR a glance.)* Yes, they will, and I'm not just saying that 'cause I'm Jean Pawlicki, your

Tupperware block sales rep. *(TRACY ANN Clap for JEAN —
JEAN awknowledge TRACY ANN with a nod or bow.)* No sir.
I too, like you, am a customer first and foremost. A satisfied
consumer that calls the strength of her Tupperware, "Tupper-
bility"...

BONNIE. How clever.

JEAN. *(To DIANE.)* That's Tupperware and durability
combined.

DIANE. Oh, I love that! Can I use it in my presenta-
tions?

JEAN. I'd be honored.

TRACY ANN. I get it, you take off the "dura" and "ware"
then you add "bility" to "Tupper".

SINCLAIR. Your mother raised no fools.

TRACY ANN. My daddy would argue that. He'd say that
my twin brothers were both fools on account'a the time they
both drank lighter fluid to get a bigger flame when lighting
their farts.

JEAN. *(Uncomfortable chuckle, quickly changing the
subject.)* That's a nice story, dear. *(Turns to DIANE.)* And
what have you brought us today, Diane?

DIANE. What have I brought you?

(She pulls out various assorted colored containers.)

TRACY ANN. I don't know.

DIANE. This is the brand new line of Tupperware which
will take us into the 70's.

TRACY ANN. It's so modern. *(The women, not SIN-
CLAIR ooh and ah.)* I have the new jello mold transporters.

TRACY ANN. I eat Jell-O constantly!

DIANE. *(The women ad lib "marvelous" "how handy" TRACY ANN: oh it's great.)* The ambrosia serving bowl

    TRACY ANN. I love ambrosia!

    DIANE. And the deviled egg carry-all.

    TRACY ANN. *(Reaches for it.)* I've got to have one! Diane can I hold it?

(DIANE ignores her.)

    JEAN. Wait, Diane, aren't we forgetting something?

(She pats the top of her head.)

    DIANE. *(Stares blankly then suddenly realizes what JEANS'S doing.)* You're right! Oh my, how can we possibly go further without putting on our Tupper hats?

    SINCLAIR. *(Sips her drink, chokes.)* Hoooold on, back it up chickee. Would you repeat that? I thought you said Tupper hats?

(DIANE starts to hand out large individual paper bags to all the ladies.)

    DIANE. Yes, I've brought you all gifts made from Tupperware products.

    TRACY ANN. I love presents.

    JEAN. Don't open your bags just yet.

    TRACY ANN. I won't.

(They wait until all but SINCLAIR'S bag is passed out.)

JEAN. Okay, open your bags.

(The ladies open their bags and giggle at the hats. The hats are made of cups, saucers, plastic fruit and plastic utensils.

SINCLAIR watches in horror as each hat is pulled from the their bags. The women's lines in this section can overlap each other.)

SINCLAIR. *(Shocked)* Christ on a cross.
TRACY ANN. These are adorable.
JEAN. I love what you've done with these ice tea spoons.
DIANE. Thank you.
TRACY ANN. It feels like Christmas.
BONNIE. I'd love to make some of these.
DIANE. I'll show you sometime.

(The ladies have put on the hats. All look at each other then to SINCLAIR.)

JEAN. Well?
SINCLAIR. Well what?
JEAN. Are you going to put yours on?

(DIANE stands over SINCLAIR holding out a large bag.)

SINCLAIR. *(You've-got-to-be-kidding-me laughter.)* No-o-o-o-o-o-o *(Extended laugh.)*
JEAN. Diane made these for us, the least you can do is wear it.

TRACY ANN. We're all wearing ours.

SINCLAIR. Well, that doesn't say much.

(They all just sit staring at her.)

SINCLAIR. *(Breaking down.)* Fine, I'll put it on.

DIANE. *(Handing SINCLAIR the bag.)* I have a special one made just for you.

SINCLAIR. And you didn't even know me.

DIANE. *(Monotone, right between the eyes.)* Oh, I do now.

(SINCLAIR pulls out the most gaudy, ridiculous looking one of them all. She reluctantly puts it on her head.)

BONNIE. It looks wonderful on you, Sinclair.

JEAN. Yes, it really brings out your eyes.

SINCLAIR. *(Looking up, hands outstretched.)* Oh Lord, I beg of thee, smite me now.

JEAN. Are we forgetting anything else?

DIANE. No, I don't think so. *(She digs through the bag to look.)* Lets see...I brought the popcicle freezing pods and the new fall line of sandwich containers...and the...

JEAN. *(Leans in, whispers.)* Aren't we forgetting to say the Tupperware motto?

TRACY ANN. *(Excited)* There's a motto?

DIANE. *(Embarrassed laugh.)* Of course. How could I forget that? I feel like a Tupper Rookie.

JEAN. *(Proudly looking at all the women.)* All the ladies have to say the Tupper motto before we begin any Tupperware party.

SINCLAIR. We do? Hold on, let me take my Tupper cyanide pill first.

(She pats herself pretending to look for the pill.)

JEAN. *(To DIANE.)* Shall I begin, Diane?

DIANE. By all means, Jean. Start the chant.

JEAN. *(Clears her throat, deep breath.)* Mr. Tupper says, "no seal seals like a Tupper seal seals".

SINCLAIR. *(In total shock by what she's witnessing.)* Oh, fer the love of Christ.

DIANE. Mr. Tupper says, "no seal seals like a Tupper seal seals".

JEAN. You all have to say it.

TRACY ANN. How fun. Mr. Tupper says, "no seal seals like a...a..." I can't say it.

DIANE. Tupper seal seals.

TRACY ANN. Too much pressure. Too much pressure.

JEAN. You can.

TRACY ANN. What if I screw it up?

SINCLAIR. You'll go to Tupper-hell.

JEAN. Just say it fast.

TRACY ANN. *(Prepares herself, breathes deep.)* Mr. Tupper says...I'm so nervous...Mr' Tupper says, "no seal seals like a Tupper seal seals". I did it!

DIANE. You did!

TRACY ANN. *(Slumps in to the chair.)* I'm exhausted.

JEAN. And now the hostess with the mostess.

BONNIE. Mr. Tupper says, "no seal seals like a Tupper seal seals".

DIANE. Right on the money.

TRACY ANN. First try.

BONNIE. It wasn't has hard as I thought it would be.

JEAN. It never is. Right girls? *(She bursts into laughter.)*
I can't believe I said that.

DIANE. Oh you, scamp.

TRACY ANN. What's that mean?

TRACY ANN. Was that a joke? Why are we laughing?

DIANE. Now you, Sinclair.

SINCLAIR. I'd rather have a car antenna shoved in my
eye.

(She calmly sips off her drink.)

JEAN. Sinclair.

BONNIE. It would be nice of you, Sinclair.

SINCLAIR. Fine. Mr. Tupper says no seal seals...Jesus
Christ, this is...

JEAN. Like a Tupper seal seals.

SINCLAIR. I got it for chrissakes!

TRACY ANN. You can do it.

SINCLAIR. *(Imitates TRACY ANN'S voice.)* I know I
can do it! *(Back to her own voice.)*.

JEAN. Then say it already.

SINCLAIR. *(Annoyed, with clenched teeth.)* I'm going
to.

TRACY ANN. *(Prodding)* Yes, say it, Sinclair.

SINCLAIR. Alright, ya Jackals! Mr. Tupper says, "no
seal seals like a Tupper seal seals". Are you happy?

DIANE. Perfect.

JEAN. See, that wasn't so difficult, was it?

SINCLAIR. I feel like I've been raped and left in a mall

parking lot. *(Removes her hat.)* Now, if there's no other dog tricks you want me to perform, can we get on with the plastic containers?

(JEAN and DIANE gasp from the words "plastic containers.".

JEAN. Tupperware. We don't call them plastic containers.

DIANE. *(Serious)* No-we-don't.

JEAN. They're Tupperware — much different from any old plastic containers.

TRACY ANN. *(Reciting it for memory.)* Tupperware. Tupperware.

(Mouthes the word as well to savior it.)

DIANE. Exactly. *(Refocuses herself.)* Now...let's start with the sandwich containers. They're dishwasher safe, virtually indestructible and come in an assortment of colors like Lime Green, Orange Rind Orange, Aztec Gold, Winter White, Peccary pink, and Boozleberry Blue.

TRACY ANN. Yum.

SINCLAIR. Boozleberry Blue? What color is Boozleberry Blue?

DIANE. It's a shade between Danish Royal Blue and Mediterranean Azure.

JEAN. ...but a shade lighter than a Venetian Violet.

BONNIE. Is it like a Blueberry Blue.

DIANE. Much lighter.

TRACY ANN. Then it's lighter than the Venetian Violet without any violet in the color?

SINCLAIR. *(Screams it out.)* IT'S BLUE! *(Then mouthes the word "Blue".)*

DIANE. *(Composes herself.)* Now, ladies, these are just a few of...

SINCLAIR. I just don't know why you didn't say blue in the first place.

JEAN. *(Loses her cool.)* Because it's Boozleberry Blue! That's the Tupper color — Boozleberry blue!

SINCLAIR. *(Yelling back at her.)* Okay, okay, I got it already!

DIANE. *(Snaps out loudly.)* HEY! *(She taps on the top of the Tupperware lid. Smiles calmly back to normal voice.)* As I was saying, these are just a few of the vast assortment of colors available to match the sandwiches you wish to preserve.

SINCLAIR. Jesus, how many sandwiches do you think I need to keep around?

BONNIE. Well it suits me just fine. I can make Richard's pastrami and the kid's peanut butter days in advance. And the color containers could keep track of which is which.

DIANE. You're catching on.

BONNIE. I'd hate to mix them up, 'cause Richard hates peanut butter. He thinks peanut butter is made from chewed up peanuts.

TRACY ANN. My Uncle Ray says the same thing! He thinks that they use old people to do the chewing. He says they tie string around their necks, so they can't swallow the peanut butter. You know, like those Japanese fishermen who tie strings around the necks of those Cormorant birds? *(TRACY ANN makes a bird with her hand and acts out the story.)*

Right? And the birds dive down in the water and they get fish and they come back up, but they can't swallow the fish 'cause the strings are tied around their necks. Much the same way the old folks can't swallow the peanut butter after they gum it.

(All are dumfounded.)

SINCLAIR. She's got the patent on crazy alright.

DIANE. *(Breaks the silence, holds up a Tupperware container.)* They're also great for dry storage or freezing foods.

BONNIE. Well, how long will they keep?

JEAN. As long as you'd like.

TRACY ANN. So I could make sandwiches weeks in advance?

SINCLAIR. Weeks?!

DIANE. Ladies, I don't have to tell you but it's my job to do so, this is the finest forms of food preservation known to science...

JEAN. ...the best.

TRACY ANN. I did not know that.

SINCLAIR. I wanna see some paper-work on that one.

DIANE. Studies prove that Tupperware locks in freshness *(Locks her hands together. JEAN follows then BONNIE and TRACY ANN do the same.)* and all the nutrition that your family needs to stay healthy.

BONNIE. Put me down for ten.

JEAN. Ten's a good round number.

(DIANE pulls out a pad to start taking orders.)

JEAN. *(CONT'D)* Mrs. Bonnie Kapica down for ten.

(Looks down at the order DIANE'S writing.)

    DIANE. What colors, dear?

    BONNIE. Well, are there any other?

    DIANE. Sure, we also have this fall: Sun Surface Yellow, Butter Brickle Beige and Rhode Island Red.

    SINCLAIR. What shade is Rhode Island Red?

    JEAN. *(Snippy)* It's Red!

    SINCLAIR. I'm just asking. Don't get all snippy on me when I'm Tupper-interested.

    BONNIE. I'll take an assortment — all except the Butter Brickle Beige. That doesn't sound real pretty.

    DIANE. Yes, it's not one of our big sellers. Neither is the Brahman Bull Brown.

    BONNIE. *(She shakes her head and gives a disgusted look.)* I don't think that color would match the stove in my kitchen. I'll take the other colors.

    JEAN. Okay then, an assortment of ten for Bonnie Kapica. Excellent — bravo!

    TRACY ANN. *(Thrusts up her hands with fingers outstretched.)* I'll take fifteen!

(Re-thrusts one hand to complete fifteen.)

    DIANE. Oh my, fifteen.

    JEAN. Bravo, that's the spirit.

    DIANE. And what colors, dear?

    TRACY ANN. I'll take an assortment, and *(Proudly)* I'll take the Butter Brickle Beige and Brahman Bull Brown.

    SINCLAIR. You would.

    TRACY ANN. Well, I don't want to seem prejudiced

against the darker colors.

SINCLAIR. Christ, it's not a Martin Luther King march on Washington.

TRACY ANN. I just like color equality.

JEAN. *(To SINCLAIR.)* And how many do you want?

SINCLAIR. *(Caught off-guard.)* Me? I don't want any of those goddam things. *(JEAN gives her an evil look.)* What? *(JEAN is unwavering. SINCLAIR breaks down.)* Fine, two.

JEAN. No, you want six — In an assortment of colors.

SINCLAIR. Is that how many I want?

JEAN. *(Determined)* Yes.

(All the women nod towards SINCLAIR at the same time.)

SINCLAIR. Okay, six.

DIANE. You won't regret it, Sinclair. These containers will make your life so much easier.

SINCLAIR. Great, I'm looking forward to it. Maybe they'll make lunches for my kids and take them to school. Hell, I could throw some wheels on them and the kids could drive themselves to school.

DIANE. I'm just saying that they'll help keep things in order.

JEAN. *(CADDY to DIANE.)* At least something will.

SINCLAIR. The queen of order speaks again.

DIANE. Well, Sinclair, Tupperware is not only changing the way women think *(Points to her head.)* in the kitchen, it's also changing the way women think about themselves. *(Points to her heart.)*

TRACY ANN. I felt that in my heart Diane.

SINCLAIR. *(To DIANE.)* Listen to you, you sound like a commercial. Do you ever listen to yourself? Huh? And now Jean here sounds like one of you Tupper zombies.

JEAN. No, I just believe in the product.

SINCLAIR. *(Skeptical)* You'd believe in a garden hose if it'd make your life less boring.

JEAN. My life is not boring.

SINCLAIR. As boring as a bowl of tapioca.

TRACY ANN. I like tapioca. I don't find tapioca boring.

SINCLAIR. That's 'cause you ARE a bowl of tapioca.

TRACY ANN. Are you saying I'm boring?

SINCLAIR. *(Announcing each syllable through her hands shaped into a bull horn.)* Bor-ing!

BONNIE. Does anyone else need a drink?

SINCLAIR. Fill up all the glasses, we'll need it for the rest of this thrill-a-minute hootenanny.

DIANE. *(Hurt by her comment, DIANE takes off her hat.)* If you didn't want me to come by then why did you ask me?

SINCLAIR. I didn't.

JEAN. I wanted you here.

BONNIE. I suggested it.

SINCLAIR. You suggested it so we could all find out who or what lives in that big Reinhart crypt.

BONNIE. That was not my intention. I was being neigh-borly.

JEAN. Exactly.

DIANE. There's nothing wrong with that house. I like that house.

TRACY ANN. Me too.

SINCLAIR. That house does nothing but suck the life out of everyone that lives there. Not one thing has ever come out of that house except bodies.

BONNIE. That's not true. *(To DIANE.)* It's not true.

DIANE. Well, I like it.

SINCLAIR. I'll give you some advice, leave the house sometime. Stop selling these containers and go out and get yourself a new husband.

JEAN. *(Takes off her hat.)* That's enough, Sinclair!

BONNIE. I agree.

TRACY ANN. That's very wrong, Sinclair.

SINCLAIR. I mean we haven't seen you come or go. Just like when old lady Reinhart lived there. She never left after her husband died either. Just like you.

BONNIE. Well, I've seen her.

DIANE. I leave the house.

SINCLAIR. When? To go do Tupperware parties?

DIANE. I leave the house.

BONNIE. Would you please leave her alone?

DIANE. I can defend myself, Bonnie.

SINCLAIR. What do you have to defend yourself from? Little old pregnant me?

TRACY ANN. Why do you have to be so mean?

SINCLAIR. I'm not mean, I'm just opening a couple Tupperware containers to see what's inside.

JEAN. It doesn't sound like it.

SINCLAIR. Sure, I want to find out about our new neighbor. Hell, I'm being neighborly, like Bonnie here.

DIANE. What do you want to know?

SINCLAIR. What do you want to tell us?

BONNIE. You don't have to say anything if you don't want to. It's your business.

JEAN. That's right, Diane, you don't. *(To SINCLAIR.)* I know enough about her. She doesn't have to answer to you.

SINCLAIR. Great, then you tell us all about her.

DIANE. I can do my own talking.

JEAN. No, please. Diane is the top sales representative for the Midwest region. That includes Illinois, Wisconsin, Iowa and parts of Michigan.

SINCLAIR. I got that. She does a real spiffy job of selling. She just got me to buy six containers. Actually, Sis, that was you that just bullied me into buying them.

DIANE. You don't have to buy anything if you don't want to.

SINCLAIR. No, huh? You're telling me that you go over to all these houses with bags of plastic just to be neighborly.

TRACY ANN. It's Tupperware, not plastic.

SINCLAIR. Hey, no matter what fancy name you label it, Tracy Ann, it's still plastic. You could spritz a pile of crap with perfume, tie a ribbon around it and paint it Boozleberry blue, but it would still be a pile of crap.

DIANE. I don't have to sell anything to be happy.

SINCLAIR. No? Then what's the use of lugging all this stuff around?

DIANE. I like meeting people.

BONNIE. Sure you do.

SINCLAIR. And now that you met us, how do you like us so far?

DIANE. You're fine.

SINCLAIR. I am? Listen to you, you don't even know when you're lying.

JEAN. Enough!

DIANE. I'm not lying.

SINCLAIR. Did your husband like this Tupperware routine? Was it salesmanship that looped him in?

JEAN. I said, enough!

BONNIE. Be civil.

SINCLAIR. I am being civil. I'm being downright neighborly.

DIANE. No, he didn't.

SINCLAIR. He didn't what?

DIANE. He didn't like my career. That's why...

SINCLAIR. Why what? C'mon spill it. We're all neighbors here.

DIANE. That's why he passed on.

SINCLAIR. You killed him with Tupperware?

DIANE. He just passed on.

SINCLAIR. Passed on. You've been a Tupper sales zombie so long you even sugar coat your own husband's death--passed on.

JEAN. Alright,knock it off!

DIANE. That's what happened.

SINCLAIR. How? Heart attack? Train wreck? Choked on a chicken bone, what?

BONNIE. *(Holds up tray of sandwiches.)* Would anybody like a sandwich — it's deviled ham — no bones.

DIANE. He passed on...me.

TRACY ANN. You don't have to talk about this Diane. We understand.

SINCLAIR. What do we understand?

TRACY ANN. We understand that he died, that's all.

DIANE. He didn't die. He left me!

BONNIE. Your husband didn't die?

DIANE. No. Four years ago he left me. *(To SINCLAIR.)* Is that what you want to hear? He passed on me and our marriage. He left me, okay? Are you happy, neighbor?

SINCLAIR. *(Laughs)* I'm giddy.

JEAN. *(Hurt)* But you told me he died.

DIANE. I never said he died. I said he passed on. It's my business. It's my embarrassment, not the world's.

JEAN. But you knew that's what I thought.

DIANE. I just never elaborated, that's all, I'm sorry.

BONNIE. *(Takes off her hat.)* You shouldn't be embarrassed that your husband left you.

TRACY ANN. He's the one that left, not you.

DIANE. He left because of me.

SINCLAIR. What's wrong with you? Hangnail? Eczema? Tupper halitosis?

BONNIE. Why does everything have to be a joke with you? Can't you see this is a serious matter?

SINCLAIR. The only serious matter I see is that Mrs. Whettlaufer — correction, Miss Whettlaufer has lied to all those around her about a dead husband.

BONNIE. It's really none of our business.

SINCLAIR. It is when I'm involved. That's a pretty intricate charade if I ever saw one.

JEAN. *(Concerned)* How long have you been lying about your husband?

DIANE. I don't know...I've lost track.

SINCLAIR. How'd you kill him off without anyone knowing?

BONNIE. This is none of our business.

JEAN. Exactly.

TRACY ANN. I'm all ears. *(All shoot her a look.)* I'm a good listener.

DIANE. *(Thinking, remembering.)* It was...it was close to Christmas...I was selling the new Tupperware Christmas wreath cookie storers like hotcakes.

BONNIE. I still have one of those.

SINCLAIR. Of course you do.

DIANE. We'd been fighting most of the fall, so Christmas didn't seem to matter much. We didn't even decorate the house that year. I came home, and Michael, that was my husband's name, Michael, was sitting by the fireplace drinking a scotch. He's not a drinker, so I knew something was a matter...He'd been crying.

TRACY ANN. *(Takes off her hat.)* He was crying?

DIANE. I never saw him do that before...So *(Distant remembering.)*...so...and I looked at him and he looked me and then he just said "no more". I knew what that meant. *(Pause)* He picked up his suitcases...and stared at me...Waiting. *(Pause)* Waiting for something he would never get — answers...maybe regrets...anything that would make him stay. *(Pause)* And...I...I said nothing. *(Regaining composure.)* And he walked out... *(Beat)* The following day I called a real estate agent, put the house up on the market and left that very same day. I told none of my neighbors I was moving...left no forwarding address. I locked the door...put the keys through the mailslot...and never looked back. *(Pause, finally realizes.)* I never said a word to him.

JEAN. And that's how he died?

DIANE. That's when he died — we died.

TRACY ANN. But you don't have to be embarrassed.

DIANE. But I am. It just got easier to say he was dead than he left me. It's embarrassing to go into home after home, full of families...and relationships...and love — you know?... and...and...tell wives that my husband left me.

JEAN. They'd understand.

DIANE. Would they? How many of those homes were the couples divorced? None. Not to many single, divorced women throw Tupperware parties. It was just easier to say he passed on. Everyone understood. No one questioned me.

JEAN. Until Sinclair opened her big fat mouth.

SINCLAIR. I was being neighborly.

TRACY ANN. You were being evil.

SINCLAIR. Aw, pipe down, farmgirl.

TRACY ANN. I will not pipe down. I'm not the one always meddling in other people's business.

SINCLAIR. I'm not the one going around letting people think that my husband is dead.

DIANE. No, I am.

SINCLAIR. See?

BONNIE. I just don't understand why you didn't tell anybody.

DIANE. Because I'm the one who drove him away. He tried to keep us together. I...gave up.

BONNIE. Why would you do that?

DIANE. Because it was easier for me. I made a career and left behind a marriage.

SINCLAIR. You threw away a marriage to sell plastic containers?

DIANE. I think I...

SINCLAIR. *(Interrupting)* You think? You think what?!

DIANE. I did.

SINCLAIR. Then you're a fool.

BONNIE. Cut it out, Sinclair.

SINCLAIR. No, she is a fool. She wanted to be some hotshot salesgirl instead of taking care of business at home.

DIANE. Yes, I did that.

SINCLAIR. Then I see nothing but a fool.

JEAN. You're not a fool.

SINCLAIR. Oh, she is. And you're an even bigger fool for thinking she's not a fool. All for some rinky-dink career in plastics.

TRACY ANN. It's Tupperware, not plastic.

SINCLAIR. See that? Ya even got the drone brain-washed.

DIANE. *(Distant, to no one in particular.)* I needed a career.

SINCLAIR. You didn't need anything. You wanted it.

DIANE. *(She nervously starts to put the containers back into their bags.)* I had to get my mind off of things.

SINCLAIR. What things? Huh? Worrying if the doilies are straight on the coffee table — if the salad containers don't burp?

DIANE. I had to forget.

SINCLAIR. No, you had to buckle down and be a wife... keep a house...have some kids. That's all. That's what we do! *(Indicates all the women.)* That's what we're supposed to do! It's called responsibility.

DIANE. I tried to be responsible.

SINCLAIR. Doesn't sound like it.

DIANE. I tried to do the right thing...to...to keep a house.. to...have children.

SINCLAIR. You obviously failed.

DIANE. *(Blows up.)* I Tried! *(Quietly)* Four times I tried for a...I couldn't try anymore. I needed to...I had to forget...I couldn't have a *(Can't say the word "Baby".)* ba...ba... *(Pause)* Every home I went into had pictures of children. Fours times I was pregnant! Four times I was going to have a...a...ba *(She finishes the word "baby" without saying a word.)* and...and then....then...then came the bleeding...and then...nothing. I couldn't try anymore! *(Quietly)* No. *(Pause — almost inaudible.)* No more. And now...I...I...have to forget...I have to.

(The ladies sit in silence while DIANE cries. She gets up and heads for the kitchen.)

DIANE. *(Cont'd)* You'll have to excuse me.
BONNIE. Let me come with you dear.

(TRACY ANN gets up to follow. She stops and looks back at SINCLAIR.)

TRACY ANN. Shame on you. Shame-on-you.
SINCLAIR. *(Feels bad but covers up.)* Yea, yea, scram, pleb.

(TRACY ANN leaves JEAN and SINCLAIR behind in silence.)

SINCLAIR. Tough break.

(JEAN stands up and searches SINCLAIR for answers to her behavior.)

JEAN. I just don't get you.

(JEAN leaves sinclair alone. A lone spotlights stays on her as the stagelights go down. SINCLAIR chugs the last of her drink.)

SINCLAIR. There's nothing to get.

CURTAIN

END OF ACT ONE

Act II

(SINCLAIR stands at the bar mixing another cocktail. She tastes the mixture then adds more vermouth to perfection.

JEAN ENTERS. She speaks to SINCLAIR in a very different tone than when she's around the other ladies — almost to SINCLAIR'S level of primal.)

JEAN. Are you happy?

SINCLAIR. You betcha, just the right amount of vermouth...ab-so-lutely perfect.

JEAN. Cut the crap you know damn well what I'm talking about.

SINCLAIR. Do I? What? Why don't you summarize exactly what I did that was so wrong.

JEAN. She's quite upset now.

SINCLAIR. Let me summarize then. May I?

JEAN. By all means.

SINCLAIR. Your perfect selling machine, has been bamboozling you and the rest of the world into thinking that her husband was dead...

JEAN. I don't care.

SINCLAIR. But oops, he's actually ditched her "A" because she's an emotional basketcase and "B" because she can't keep a baby alive long enough to bring it to fruition.

JEAN. I didn't know you could be so cruel.

SINCLAIR. Life's cruel, Jean. It's survival of the fittest and I'm just plucking out the weak calves from the heard.

(Pulls an olive out of her martini and eats it.)

JEAN. D'you know what I think?

SINCLAIR. I don't care.

JEAN. I think you're just one of those weak calves in wolf's clothing — that's what I think. And mark my words, one day someone bigger and meaner is gonna come along and knock-you-down.

SINCLAIR. That'll be tough.

JEAN. And then I'm just gonna stand back and laugh my ass off...laugh 'til I pee my pants.

SINCLAIR. I can take care of myself.

JEAN. Well try taking care of someone else once. Feel something for once. Of all the mean and nasty stunts you've pulled, I can honestly say that today takes the cake. You're officially the biggest bully on the block.

SINCLAIR. I'm a success then.

JEAN. You're just so damn angry. Every year you just get worse. But today...today... you...you...*(Frustrated, realizes that it's not worth the fight.)* just leave her alone — leave us all alone.

SINCLAIR. Why should I?

JEAN. Because she's done nothing to you...the world's done nothing to Sinclair Benevente.

SINCLAIR. Really?

JEAN. Really. And as your sister and Friend, maybe the last one at the rate you're going, I'm asking you to lay off for the rest of the evening — please.

SINCLAIR. I don't see why I —

JEAN. PLEASE!

SINCLAIR. Fine, I don't want to ruin my buzz anyway.

JEAN. Good. And I want you to apologize to her.

SINCLAIR. For what?! Huh? Now I'm the bad guy? All I did was expose her.

JEAN. It's not your job.

SINCLAIR. Well someone's gotta do it.

JEAN. But not you, and not tonight. Do this for me, okay? *(SINCLAIR doesn't respond.)* Sinclair, this is really important to me.

SINCLAIR. *(Sits back with her legs open.)* You're lucky I like you.

JEAN. Well, I don't like you right now. *(Beat)* And lay off the booze.

SINCLAIR. What? It's the only reason that I've survived with this Coney Island Freakshow as long as I have. Make a choice...apology or no booze.

JEAN. Both.

BONNIE. *(O.S.)* No, I'm sorry about this whole mess. Diane...

SINCLAIR. Pick one *(She cups her ear.)* I think I hear them coming back.

JEAN. I want an apology. *(Realizes SINCLAIR'S legs are open and reaches over and slams them shut.)* Keep 'em closed, you're attracting flies.

(BONNIE RETURNS with DIANE.)

DIANE. No, I really think I should be going. You've been a gracious host. I hope we can do this again sometime.

BONNIE. No, please stay. It'll be fine.

DIANE. No, it won't.

JEAN. Diane, please, you can't leave. Were just getting started.

SINCLAIR. *(Under her breath.)* Yes, we are.

(JEAN overhears the comment and shoots her a stifling glance.)

JEAN. We haven't seen the popcicle freezer pods or the deviled egg carriers, or...or...the...

DIANE. Maybe some other time.

BONNIE. I'd really like to see that deviled egg carrier though.

JEAN. See, she wants to see the deviled egg carriers. Besides Sinclair wants to say something to you.

SINCLAIR. Do I?

DIANE. I think it's better that I leave.

JEAN. Not before Sinclair says something very important. Right, Sinclair?

SINCLAIR. Nothing comes to mind.

JEAN. Sinclair!

SINCLAIR. Fine. Diane, about what I said earlier...

JEAN. Go on.

SINCLAIR. Yea, well, I just wanted to say that I'm...

(TRACY ANN sashays into the room carrying a tray full of individual glass serving dishes filled with chocolate pudding and a dollop of cool whip on top.)

TRACY ANN. *(Interrupting)* Who wants pudding?!

SINCLAIR. *(Facetiously towards JEAN.)* Pudding, I love pudding!

JEAN. Now's not the right time for pudding, Tracy Ann.

TRACY ANN. It's always the right time for pudding.

SINCLAIR. I agree, Jean.

JEAN. *(Less patient, still trying to maintain control.)* No really, we should have pudding later.

TRACY ANN. By then there'll be pudding skin on top.

BONNIE. It's instant. There shouldn't be any pudding skin on top. I followed directions on the packet. I'll show you.

(BONNIE LEAVES to get the packet of pudding.)

SINCLAIR. Nothing worse than that pudding skin, Jean.

JEAN. *(Even less patience.)* Not right now.

TRACY ANN. But I just put the Cool Whip on top!

SINCLAIR. She just put the Cool Whip on top, Sis.

JEAN. *(Growling)* Put the pudding back in the fridge!

TRACY ANN. But it's all ready.

SINCLAIR. *(Resounding agreement.)* But it's all ready.

JEAN. Tracy Ann, put the damn pudding back right now!

(Defeated, TRACY ANN doesn't say a word and abruptly turns to leave with tray in tow. BONNIE ENTERS with the packet and hands it to JEAN.)

BONNIE. See? Right on the packet — instant.

JEAN. *(Cont'd without looking frazzled.)* I see. *(Calmly gathering her wits.)* Now then, where were we?

SINCLAIR. That pudding sure looked good, Bon.

BONNIE. It was Dutch Chocolate.

SINCLAIR. My favorite. Maybe we should re-think the pudding. Whadda ya say, girls?

JEAN. No pudding! You were going to say something to Diane.

SINCLAIR. I was? *(JEAN gives the look.)* I was going to say, I'm...about earlier.

DIANE. Maybe it was about time I faced up to this situation. Just the same, I think I should leave.

BONNIE. Nonsense, we still want to see the rest of the fall line. Right, Sinclair? *(Waits for an answer.)* Right?

SINCLAIR. *(Acquiesces)* Wild horses couldn't drag me outta here...

BONNIE. See that?

SINCLAIR. Even with ropes binding my ankles and dragging me over hot coals...

JEAN. Fine, That's...

SINCLAIR. And mounds of tacks and bits of glass...

JEAN. *(Frustrated)* We get it! *(Calms herself.)* What she's trying to say in her own demented way is, she wants you to stay.

DIANE. *(Trying to regain her dignity.)* Well, if you'd go through all that to keep me here, then I guess I'll have to stay.

SINCLAIR. But no more hats.

DIANE. No more hats.

(TRACY ANN sadly ENTERS slumped and broken.)

TRACY ANN. *(Flustered)* Well, don't blame me later if the Cool whip rolls off and the pudding has skin! Dagnamitt, I tried!

JEAN. And we appreciate it.

TRACY ANN. Well it bothers me, okay, Jean? *(To DI-ANE.)* I see this thing all the time at the hospital, I know.

DIANE. What's that?

TRACY ANN. I volunteer at St. Mary Magdalene's Hosptial for the indigent and infirmed. *(SINCLAIR groans.)* When I serve the patients their meals sometimes I notice that the pudding has skin on it. *(Becoming more upset.)* And... and...and I figure that these poor people may have just gotten out of having a...a... gallbladder removed or...or...or'a brainadectomy or something...and...and the last thing that they need is pudding with skin on it! So before I serve it I-peel-the-skin-off. *(Breaks into sobbing.)*

(JEAN and BONNIE rush over to comfort her.)

JEAN. There, there.

TRACY ANN. *(Lightly sobbing and sniffling.)* I just don't want pudding skin...I just don't like it.

BONNIE. The pudding wouldn't have skin on it was instant.

SINCLAIR. *(Facetious)* Boy, you're a regular Florence Nightingale.

TRACY ANN. *(Calming herself.)* Yes, well, I try to make their stay as pleasant as possible.

DIANE. That's nice.

SINCLAIR. So you don't talk to them then?

DIANE. *(Friendly but firm.)* Sinclair.

TRACY ANN. When?

SINCLAIR. When you're serving them. I'm sure not talking to them would make their stay as pleasant as possible.

TRACY ANN. I'm just going to ignore that comment. I didn't even hear it.

JEAN. Good for you.

SINCLAIR. Yes, good for you. *(Points to TRACY ANN.)* Laufer That's the one who needs the brainadectomy.

TRACY ANN. Diane, I surely could use one of those deviled egg carriers alright, Diane.

JEAN. Sure you could.

TRACY ANN. Last summer I brought some deviled eggs to my family reunion. And the paper plate got all soggy and the eggs ended up in my little cousin Regi's sandbox.

SINCLAIR. I'll bet it improved their flavor.

TRACY ANN. You'd have to ask the dogs. They ate 'em and their poop smelled like paprika for a week. Surprisingly fragrant.

JEAN. *(Uncomfortable JEAN laugh.)* Let's get back to the matter at hand.

DIANE. Yes, the matter at hand. The new deviled egg carriers.

JEAN. Ta da.

TRACY ANN. *(Raises her hand.)* I'll take one!

DIANE. I haven't gone into the specs of the deviled egg carry-all yet.

TRACY ANN. Anything that will keep the dogs from eating my deviled eggs is number one on my shopping list.

DIANE. As they should be. As a matter of fact these carriers will keep your eggs fresh all day. Or you can use it to preserve anything that needs preserving.

BONNIE. They preserve things that good?

TRACY ANN. Speaking of preserving...

JEAN. *(Drops her head in her hands.)* Oh, Christ.

TRACY ANN. ...One time my brother Billy put a toad in the freezer and forgot about it. He found it two years later. It was covered in ice and stiff as a...a...

SINCLAIR. Frozen toad?

TRACY ANN. Yes, as stiff as a frozen toad...and he threw the frozen toad off the roof and when it hit the driveway it shattered into a million tiny, frozen toad pieces.

DIANE. That's terrible.

JEAN. Tragic.

TRACY ANN. Yes, it was. Then he tried to glue all the pieces back together, but it never did quite look like a toad again. *(She slightly contorts herself into a mime of a disfigured toad.)* I guess he was missing some pieces.

SINCLAIR. I'm sure you wouldn't have had that problem if he put it in one of these Tupperware containers.

TRACY ANN. I suppose not. *(To DIANE who's not really paying attention.)* Diane, Diane, DIANE! Would the toad have been preserved if it was in one of these containers?

(All the women turn to DIANE in anticipation of the answer.)

DIANE. Well, I'm not sure. I suppose so.
JEAN. I suppose so.
TRACY ANN. It's a miracle
JEAN. Yes, it's a miracle.

BONNIE. Say they built one of those Tupperware containers big enough to fit me. Would I be preserved?

DIANE. *(Laughing, thinking it's a joke.)* Well, you'd suffocate, Bonnie.

JEAN. Why are you asking this, dear?

BONNIE. Well, tonight Richard told me that I don't look like I did twenty years ago.

SINCLAIR. Well, you don't.

JEAN. Shut up, Sinclair! *(Calmly to BONNIE.)* I can't believe he'd say that to you.

DIANE. That's a terrible thing to say to a woman.

SINCLAIR. The bastard. I say we rip his balls off and put them in sandwich container. I'll donate one of mine.

TRACY ANN. Aging is such a sore subject in a marriage.

BONNIE. What do you know? You just got married two months ago.

TRACY ANN. So, what's that got to do with it?

BONNIE. So your looks haven't faded yet.

SINCLAIR. You don't have a wrinkle on you. And look at you, you probably don't even need to wear a bra.

TRACY ANN. I wear a bra.

SINCLAIR. Yea, but look at those things. They stand straight up like rockets. You're gonna poke somebody's eye out someday.

TRACY ANN. They're not that firm. *(Proudly laughs to herself and struts back to her chair.)*

SINCLAIR. And you're still thin as a goddam rail. Look't you, you still have an identifiable waist.

TRACY ANN. So do you. *(Looks at her bulging waist.)* Kinda.

BONNIE. And your husband still looks at you...like Richard used to look at me.

TRACY ANN. I'm sure that's not true.

BONNIE. No? Well your husband didn't just tell you that you don't look good anymore, now did he?!

TRACY ANN. I'm sure he didn't mean it.

BONNIE. If he said it, he meant it.

SINCLAIR. That's Richard alright. The prick.

TRACY ANN. Maybe he didn't mean it like you heard.

BONNIE. He did. I know what I heard. I know what I feel, I know I'm not beautiful anymore.

JEAN. You're wrong, Bonnie.

DIANE. Very wrong.

TRACY ANN. You're still beautiful.

BONNIE. Oh, am I? I know is my husband doesn't take a second look at me anymore — no man does.

JEAN. I'm sure they do.

BONNIE. No, they don't! They don't. And my husband... my husband...he looks at...he looks at other women--younger ones. At the check out girls at the market, The popcorn girls at the movies...my son's girlfriend.

JEAN. *(Somewhat horrified.)* No.

SINCLAIR. The pervert.

BONNIE. He does. They all do. All your husbands look too. *(To JEAN.)* I've seen your husband look at Tracy Ann.

TRACY ANN. What?

BONNIE. *(To JEAN.)* You know what I'm talking about.

JEAN. He does? When?

BONNIE. I saw him last year at the beach, at the labor day picnic. She was wearing that hot two-piece suit...

JEAN. That's right, the blue two-piece with the dandelions on them.

TRACY ANN. They were daisies.

SINCLAIR. Yeah you wore that napkin, and i was wearing enough fabric to double as an extermination tent.

JEAN. *(Remembers)* Yep. The men were straining their eyes to watch you slather on that Coppertone Oil.

TRACY ANN. I wasn't trying to do anything.

SINCLAIR. You should'a just poured gravy all over yourself and rang the damn dinner bell.

TRACY ANN. I don't like gravy.

BONNIE. Well, men do.

SINCLAIR. Maybe she's after all our husbands.

TRACY ANN. *(Huge laughter.)* I am not.

JEAN. Don't worry about it. I can't lie to myself. I'm sure he looked. *(Feigns a joke.)* I guess sometimes eyes wander...

SINCLAIR. Only *his* eyes?

JEAN. *(Shoots her a look.)* What's that supposed to mean?

SINCLAIR. You know exactly what it means.

JEAN. No, I don't.

SINCLAIR. There's unrest in the palace of Jean. The king has been busy tending to his flock.

JEAN. Shut up.

SINCLAIR. While the queen sits alone on the throne.

BONNIE. What's she talking about, Jean?

SINCLAIR. What am I talking about, Jean?

JEAN. *(Leans in close to SINCLAIR in a loud fast whisper.)* I tell you one thing in private and now you have to throw it back in my face.

SINCLAIR. Seems fair or should I say affair? oops
BONNIE. Is she saying what I think she's saying?

(JEAN looks away.)

TRACY ANN. What's she saying?
DIANE. Jean's husband is having an affair.
TRACY ANN. Nooo.
JEAN. I'm pretty sure.
TRACY ANN. But I thought your marriage was perfect.
SINCLAIR. Nope, cat's out of the bag.
JEAN. Is that a joke to you? Is it funny that this is hap-
pening? *(SINCLAIR sees her pain and doesn't respond.)* Huh?
(SINCLAIR looks away.) Well it's not to me.
BONNIE. Do you know who it is?
JEAN. One of his assistants. I found out at an office par-
ty. I didn't want to but I did. *(Pause)* I mean...I spent Two
hours at the beauty parlor. A manicure, a pedicure, wore my
new dress.
BONNIE. Which one?
JEAN. The red one with the chiffon sleeves.
BONNIE. That one is gorgeous.
JEAN. And it cuts two inches off my hips...*(Distant quietly.)* yep two whole inches and still he...So, there I was red
dress and all and I thought...I really thought that I looked just
right... but... *(Pause)* We walked into the party, and there were
other women — wives...like me. And just like me, I'm sure
the same amount of time was spent looking the way we did.
(Remembering) And then — then...roaming the room...were...
gaggles of girls...half my age...they were — flawless...and...
and — radiant and fresh. And all around those giggling girls

were hoards of men drooling all over them. And I turned back to my husband to...and he *(She starts to well up.)*...he was now staring at them — at her. That one. He had that look in his eyes...and she was looking at him the same way. It was just for a moment...and I...knew. *(Pauses, crushed by the thought.)* Everything I had done to look good that day...everything I thought I was, melted away when I saw that. In seconds I became invisible and I felt...*No* I knew I was beaten.

DIANE. You're not beaten.

JEAN. But I'm not winning either.

TRACY ANN. Why don't you leave him?

JEAN. Because...because he's my husband.

SINCLAIR. Well, at least you're rich.

JEAN. Yes, but I can't buy back his stares.

TRACY ANN. Well, I'd leave him.

BONNIE. Sometimes you can't. The more years you've invested the harder it is. So enjoy it now, 'cause one day things may change. You'll lose that new car look and smell, then you'll realize that there are no more second glances in your direction...

DIANE. No more whistles when you pass by.

BONNIE. *(Distant, thinking about the loss of whistles, attention.)* Yep...And...and Faster and faster it will all coming apart Tracy Ann. I've pulled it up and tied it back then fastened it down. I'm dropping and drooping and stretching and hanging and bulging...and...and...I'm drying up in places that used to be wet! *(Flat to the other women.)* And I don't even drink gin! *(Pause, quietly.)* I just want to recognize the person in the mirror. I'd like to have back my youth. I'd like to have me back.

SINCLAIR. I've got a beauty tip — Twinkees — and lots of them. The fatter I get, the younger my face looks. If I lose any weight, the loose skin would add forty years of wrinkles to me. Bloated works.

TRACY ANN. It's probably why corpses that have been floating in a lake for a week always look so youthful.

DIANE. Anyone up for a swim?

BONNIE. Tracy Ann will wear her dandelion suit and depress us all over again.

TRACY ANN. They were daises.

JEAN. Well keep the suit 'cause my husband likes it.

SINCLAIR. Hell, not even a zit-faced stock boy will jump to his feet to help me find the dandruff shampoo.

(The women pause to reflect.)

JEAN. *(Breaking the mood.)* And sadly, then you realize that you've become Sinclair.

(All the women break out into uncomfortable laughter.)

SINCLAIR. Men admire my fertility.

JEAN. You wish.

SINCLAIR. Hey, I'm fully aware I don't get those animal stares. I never have. I've learned to accept it. My body's been stretched from one end to the other. My tits look like one of those topless Zulu women in a National Geographic magazine. I gotta an ass with more dimples than a room full of smiling first graders.

JEAN. Why do you have to be so crass?

SINCLAIR. I'm not being crass. I'm being a realist. I'm not gonna fool myself into wishing I would or could be fawned over. I know I'll never be as perky and giddy as this little chippy. *(Indicating TRACY ANN.)*

TRACY ANN. What's a chippy?

JEAN. You.

TRACY ANN. Well, what does that mean?

SINCLAIR. A floozy, a bimbo, get it?

TRACY ANN. I am not a bimbo!

BONNIE. She's not a bimbo. A chippy maybe — not a bimbo.

TRACY ANN. Look, I can't help it how old I am or how I look. It doesn't make me a chippy or a floozy or a bimbo.

BONNIE. No, it doesn't.

TRACY ANN. Besides, the women in my family age well. It's in the genes. I'll have you know that when my mother was 60 she looked thirty-five. I think I'll probably look much better at your age.

(All the women look up at the audience.)

BONNIE. Somebody kill her.

DIANE. I second that motion.

SINCLAIR. Yea, let's kill the bimbo.

TRACY ANN. Take that back!

SINCLAIR. What are you gonna do?

TRACY ANN. I'm gonna do plenty, you...you...pregnant sow!

SINCLAIR. Well the bimbo has grown some balls, huh? *(Leans over towards TRACY ANN.)* Listen, ya little freak, d'ya want me to knock those balls back to Steamboat Boulder, Idaho?

TRACY ANN. Steamboat Rock, Iowa! Iowa! Iowa! Iowa!

SINCLAIR. Fine, I'll knock you back to one of those inbred states.

BONNIE. Alright, ladies, let's not get vicious.

SINCLAIR. This isn't vicious. I'm not vicious. I'm preg...

DIANE. *(Matter-of-factly, under her breath.)* Oh, you're vicious alright.

SINCLAIR. Excuse me? *(DIANE doesn't answer.)* What did you say?

DIANE. I didn't say anything.

JEAN. Oh, Jesus, leave her alone.

SINCLAIR. I thought I heard the Tupperware lady say something.

BONNIE. She didn't say anything.

SINCLAIR. No, I definitely heard something. Or are you gonna hide behind your little plastic containers now?

DIANE. *(Gathering defiance.)* I said...you can be vicious.

SINCLAIR. *(Pause, take a beat.)* I'm allowed to be vicious, I'm pregnant. Pregnant people are allowed to be vicious. Particularly pregnant people who've had four, count 'em, one-two-three-four healthy babies.

BONNIE. Sinclair!

SINCLAIR. *(Flaunts her belly.)* Oh, and I have another one on the way.

DIANE. You know what? I don't need this.

(DIANE begins to put away her tupperware to leave.)

JEAN. Damitt, Sinclair!

SINCLAIR. Go ahead, gather your little plastic life together and hike on down to that big empty house.

BONNIE. Stop it Sinclair. Diane, I'm so sorry.

SINCLAIR. Don't apologize to her. You didn't do anything. And neither will she. She'll live in the big empty Reinhart place, just like old lady Reinhart did. And she'll die in the Reinhart place just like old lady Reinhart...alone.

JEAN. Stop it, Sinclair!

SINCLAIR. And then, when you're cold in the ground, buried in a massive coffin made of Tupperware, in a grave marked with a Tupperware tombstone, will they then, and only then, call it old lady Whettlaufer's place. And then a new Tupperware lady will move in...husbandless...without children...and the cycle will go on.

DIANE. You're a goddam animal.

SINCLAIR. Yes, I'm a wolf. And you, Miss Diane, are nothing but a calf to be weeded out of the herd.

DIANE. I'm a calf? Think again. I'm the top in my field — I'm...I'm the best. More wolf than you'll ever hope to be.

SINCLAIR. Keep tossing pennies in that wishing well, sweetheart.

DIANE. What? You think you're better because you can have children and keep a husband? That make you better? Is that the best you've got?

SINCLAIR. Oh there's always more, honey.

DIANE. What else have you ever done, huh? Please, name it.

SINCLAIR. I've done plenty. I've done plenty!

DIANE. What? Did you write a book? Win the Pulitzer prize? Find a cure for cancer? What? Come on, what have you done besides procreate? Huh Huh?!? *(SINCLAIR is speechless she's frozen in thought.)* Just as I thought...nothing.

(DIANE turns to leave.)

DIANE. *(Cont'd, over her shoulder.)* Good night, ladies. It's been swell.

SINCLAIR. Don't you turn your back on me! I've done plenty! I...I have a husband...I have children!

DIANE. But what else have you done? What else are you?

SINCLAIR. I'm not you! I have a husband and...and... and...my damn children. And another one on the way — again.

DIANE. Well, aren't you lucky.

SINCLAIR. Lucky? I'm lucky? Let me tell you it's not all it's cracked up to be. You got out lucky.

DIANE. Why am I lucky?

SINCLAIR. Because you don't have what I have. Ya know...not every woman wants a child. Just because we can have them doesn't mean we should.

BONNIE. That's not true.

SINCLAIR. It is. We don't have to. Why? Right? I mean is the pay off that great? Really? Is it?

BONNIE. I think so.

TRACY ANN. It's the most beautiful thing in the world.

SINCLAIR. *(She looks at her belly.)* You call this beautiful?

TRACY ANN. Yes, of course.

SINCLAIR. *(Becoming more angry.)* Is this cute to you? Is this some cute little toy to you, huh? Something to play with? Show your friends? Well, not to me. This *(Points to her belly.)*...this is eighteen years of responsibility stretching me out. Eighteen years shackled to a walking anchor...you want to trade your life for this?

TRACY ANN. Yes, I would.

SINCLAIR. I'm serious. There is no more Tracy Ann after it's born. You are it's keeper. All this has done is made me uglier. So where's my pay off? Huh? What do I get for trading me in?

JEAN. You get the love of your children.

SINCLAIR. *(More angry.)* Oh Bullshit! I sure as hell missed that perk.

BONNIE. But you love your children.

SINCLAIR. *(Blind anger.)* I hate my children!

BONNIE. Don't say that. You don't mean it.

SINCLAIR. I wanted more than this. I was creative. I had a mind. *(Tapping on her skull.)* There was something here...something else...something great. *(Pause)* But no, no... and now...now every time I get pregnant, d'you know what I wanna do, huh? *(Calm and monotone.)* I wanna fall belly first on a rake.

TRACY ANN. No, Sinclair.

JEAN. Take-that-back.

SINCLAIR. Yes, I do. Belly first. I have nightmares about my children all the time. And get this, some of my dreams involve the remote chance that this one *(Indicating the baby.)* won't live so there's not one more to take care of...

BONNIE. Stop this right now!

SINCLAIR. No! No. Everything I have in my pathetic little house has been broken by them or my husband. They've taken what I could have been. *(Pause)* You're lucky, Bonnie. You're lucky that your husband doesn't want to screw you anymore. That's the only way mine knows how to show any emotion at all. He comes home whiskey stinkin' drunk and gets on top of me. Would you like that, Bonnie? Huh? Oh, he'll pay attention to you alright. You could be Mrs. Frankie Benevente, wife of a gas station grease monkey. You can have the grease that's caked under his nails digging around inside you. Huh? Sounds good? *(Pauses, shaking with anger.)* And as a bonus, he leaves his work shirt on while he's screwing you and you get to watch the embroidered name "Frankie" coming at you back and forth and back and forth while he grunts and wheezes like a fuckin' animal! *(Pauses, then sadly.)* And the sad thing — the pathetic moral of the story is that you'll appreciate it, Bonnie, yep because it's the only time he'll ever pay attention to you anyway.

JEAN. Calm down, Sinclair.

SINCLAIR. Calm down?! Listen to you — calm down. You-piss-me-off. Your rich husband, your big house, your magic life. Don't tell me to calm down.

JEAN. My life is not perfect.

SINCLAIR. Your husband's whore confirmed that.

(JEAN slaps SINCLAIR. SINCLAIR hardly flinches or loses a beat.)

SINCLAIR. Or are you the real whore?

JEAN. SHUT UP!

(JEAN once again attempts to swing at SINCLAIR but SIN-CLAIR grabs her wrist in mid swing.)

SINCLAIR. You got the first one for free *(She tightens her opposite fist and brings it up slightly into JEAN'S field of view.)* the second one's gonna cost ya.

JEAN. *(She pulls away.)* Don't push it.

(JEAN backs away a few steps — SINCLAIR and JEAN have a momentary face off. Then JEAN turns around.)

SINCLAIR. Tough to lose it when your used to getting it all. Huh? When everything's had your name embroidered on it. All our parent's attention...all their compliments...all their love...

JEAN. That's not true, they loved you.

SINCLAIR. They tolerated me!

JEAN. That's not my fault!

SINCLAIR. Oh no? Well no one could find me in your illustrious shadow. No, No, I was nothing but Sinclair the pig, the town slut. Remember? The one that was hard on the eyes but easy in the sack. Right? RIGHT?!

JEAN. I never ever thought of you like that.

SINCLAIR. You never ever thought of me at all! *(Pause)* You got the best, while I got all the drunks and the rejects and the left overs. And that's what I have now — the goddam scraps.

DIANE. *(Compassionately)* But Sinclair, I'm sure you have a...

SINCLAIR. What? What do I have? You don't know what I have. Don't get all nice with me. Don't you dare. You...I could've been you. I could have had a career. Don't even pity me. This is who I am. This is what I was meant to be.

(SINCLAIR begins to feel a pain in her abdomen.)

TRACY ANN. Stop it, Sinclair.

SINCLAIR. Shut the hell up, you pathetic little farmgirl. *(Breathes a little heaver because of the pain.)* And while I'm chumming my guts all over the room, if I have to hear your squeaky little voice anymore, I'll shoot myself! *(The pain is getting much worse.)* Every time you speak, I want to stick a pencil in my ear and grind out my brain so I don't have to hear anymore about you and your inbred clan of sideshow freaks. *(The pain is excruciating.)* You and those ridiculous tales of your...your...*(She starts to get dizzy.)* Of...oh shit...shit...*(She grabs her stomach.)* Jesus Christ...I think...ooooohhh!

BONNIE. What's wrong?

SINCLAIR. *(Breathing heavy.)* I think...I'm going into... la...

JEAN. She's going into labor!

TRACY ANN. She's going to have the baby?!

JEAN. That's what it looks like.

DIANE. Sit down.

TRACY ANN. But here? Now?

JEAN. Babies have their own agenda.

SINCLAIR. *(Breathing heavy, grunting.)* Ooooooh Christ... not again.

TRACY ANN. Call an ambulance.

JEAN. *(Grabs SINCLAIR.)* I think it's going to be too late. Lay her flat.

SINCLAIR. Get your hands offa me!
BONNIE. Lay her on the couch.
JEAN. Not the couch that's your new upholstery.
BONNIE. Oh, that's right. *(Looks around thinking.)* Lay her on the coffee table. I'll re dust later.

(They lay SINCLAIR down on the coffee table sideways with her feet in missionary position.)

DIANE. What can I do?
SINCLAIR. Get me a drink.
JEAN. No booze. Bonnie, get her underwear off.
BONNIE. Why me?!
JEAN. Get in there!

(BONNIE reaches under SINCLAIR'S dress and proceeds to pull off her underwear. She hands them to TRACY ANN. TRACY ANN holds them up wide and is devastated, amazed by their size.)

BONNIE. We need some hot water and towels.

(BONNIE rushes out of the room.)

JEAN. Good thinking.
DIANE. What can I do?
JEAN. Hold her head up. Tracy Ann, Get me something to put the baby in when he comes out.
TRACY ANN. *(Panicked)* What?
JEAN. I don't know. Look around for something.
TRACY ANN. What should I get?

JEAN. Anything!
TRACY ANN. Where should I look?!
JEAN. Around!
TRACY ANN. Okay!

(TRACY ANN scampers about the room looking for something. She heads for the bar. TRACY ANN grabs a martini glass and ice tongs and runs back to JEAN.)

JEAN. I don't think her water has broken.
DIANE. That's the best news I've heard all day.
JEAN. I second that...

(TRACY ANN holds out the martini glass and clicks the ice tongs.)

JEAN. What the hell is that?!
TRACY ANN. *(Realizing what she's holding.)* I don't know.

(TRACY ANN runs back to the bar drops off the martini glass and grabs the deviled egg carrier on the way back. She still holds the ice tongs. BONNIE rushes in with towels.)

BONNIE. How's it coming?
JEAN. I don't see anything.
BONNIE. Well, what do you see?
JEAN. Someone who needs to shave once in a while.

(TRACY ANN looks under SINCLAIR'S dress. She is horrified to say the least.)

TRACY ANN. *(To JEAN.)* Maybe I should go get your shag rake.

SINCLAIR. Yea, go get it, so I can rap it upside your pea brain.

JEAN. She's not dilated, I don't see anything.

(Suddenly SINCLAIR lets out a earth shattering fart. They all stare at her.)

SINCLAIR. *(Much calmer.)* Huh...The pain's all gone.

DIANE. That's it? She had nothing but gas?

JEAN. Nothing but gas.

(DIANE drops SINCLAIR'S head. The women disperse among the room and sit back exhausted leaving sinclair alone on the coffee table.)

TRACY ANN. That's it? You just tooted?

SINCLAIR. It felt like labor. *(She sits up.)* Much better.

JEAN. Good, I'm glad at least you're happy now.

BONNIE. All that for gas?

SINCLAIR. Yea, well...must've been that baked ziti I had last night. Boy, that stuff'll come back and haunt you with a vengeance, huh?

(The ladies ignore her.)

SINCLAIR *(Cont'd)* All that cheese and garlic just sits there boiling up — wait'n to come out. *(Looking at the ladies.)* Then whammo...*(She looks around the room.)* Is anyone gonna help me offa here? *(No reaction.)* Fine, I'll just roll off myself. *(She realizes her underwear is gone.)* Can someone get me my underwear? *(No one moves.)* Please?

(TRACY ANN reluctantly uses her ice tongs to slowly pick up the massive panties. She holds them in front of SINCLAIR. SINCLAIR snatches them off the tongs, waddles off the table and pulls them on.)

SINCLAIR. I get it — the silent treatment. So you're all pissed at me, huh?

JEAN. You crossed the line this time.

SINCLAIR. It just came out.

TRACY ANN. It was wrong.

JEAN. I'm sorry you feel this way. Obviously this is something that has been boiling up inside you for quite sometime.

DIANE. Well apparently, it was the ziti.

JEAN. Besides all that, I've always thought highly of you. I've always respected you — until now.

SINCLAIR. *(Looking around the room.)* Bonnie, could you get me...

BONNIE. *(Interrupting)* Don't! I'm...I'm just so angry at you right now. I'm appalled at what you said about your children. How could any human being with any decency actually hate her children.

SINCLAIR. Listen, I meant...

BONNIE. *(Getting fired up.)* I don't want to hear another word out of you. Say one more thing and I'm going to...to... punch you in the mouth! How could you say such a thing? I know that it's been difficult for you, but you have to do the best you can with what you got...what we got. And you make the best of it with honor, and love and a sense of decency. I believe that the lord puts these barriers in our way for a reason. I also believe he gives us the tools to deal with these barriers and that's friends and family and children too. You don't talk to your friends the way you just did or your sister for that matter. You treat people the way you want to be treated. Especially those who care about you!

SINCLAIR. *(Interrupting)* Maybe I don't say things right...

BONNIE. *(Even more angry.)* I'm not finished! *(She picks up a large ashtray.)* Don't make me break your jaw with this ashtray! Listen to me, if I ever hear you say that about your children again...so help me...If you don't want your baby then give it to me. I'll adopt it. I'm not kidding, I'll take it, and If you don't want your other children I'll take them as well!

JEAN. Even the one who eats grass?

BONNIE. I'll give him three meals a day full of grass if that's what makes him happy. If I ever — ever, hear you utter those words...so help me...you'll...*(Overwhelmed with anger.)* you'll be sipping your meals through a straw! *(She pauses, realizes she feels empowered, stands taller.)* There, I've said my peace. I need a drink.

(The women are impressed by BONNIE'S outburst — they reflect in silence a beat until...)

DIANE. *(Quietly)* I'll adopt one of your children, Sinclair. *(All women turn to her.)* Really, I have plenty of space. *(She touches her heart.)*

BONNIE. *(Touched, quietly.)* Of course you do.

SINCLAIR. *(She is noticeably touched.)* I don't want to...it's just that...all those kids just wear me down.

BONNIE. Yes, they do. It takes hard work and self sacrifice to produce decent human beings.

SINCLAIR. I'm sorry.

BONNIE. Don't apologize to me. Apologize to everyone who was worried about you when they thought you were going into labor.

SINCLAIR. Yea, I know.

BONNIE. Do it!

SINCLAIR. Jean you know about what I said, I'm sorry about your husband and...

JEAN. Don't worry about it.

SINCLAIR. Diane, I...

DIANE. Maybe we shouldn't drink at Tupperware parties?

SINCLAIR. Yea.

(She turns to TRACY ANN but just waves her away.)

TRACY ANN. Well, I want to hear an apology.

SINCLAIR. *(Almost turning on her.)* Listen, you little shit...

BONNIE. *(Reproachfully)* Sinclair!

SINCLAIR. I was going to say, listen you little bundle of joy, I'm sorry about what I said.

TRACY ANN. Even the part about me being a pathetic farmgirl?

SINCLAIR. I love agriculture.

TRACY ANN. Even the part about wanting to stick a pencil in your ear when I tell my stories?

SINCLAIR. *(Looks at BONNIE.)* I love your stories.

TRACY ANN. How about...

SINCLAIR. Don't push you're luck.

TRACY ANN. Okay.

JEAN. Maybe we should look at some more Tupperware.

DIANE. Maybe we shouldn't.

JEAN. You're probably right. I suppose the mood has changed a bit.

DIANE. Just a tad.

TRACY ANN. So what does everyone want to do now?

DIANE. Maybe we should just relax awhile.

BONNIE. Yes, maybe we should.

JEAN. Maybe my life is as boring as tapioca. Maybe I do need something else.

TRACY ANN. But what?

JEAN. I don't know. I never thought about it before. I guess there's got to be something more to life than being a housewife. I mean, what are we doing with our lives?

DIANE. *(Disappointed by her own reality.)* We're sitting around talking about plastic.

TRACY ANN. It's Tupperware, not plastic.

DIANE. It's plastic. We're sitting around talking about plastic.

BONNIE. Well, this is better than being one of those doped-up hippie women who burn their bras in the street.

JEAN. *(Stands up excited.)* That's it!

BONNIE. What's it?

JEAN. That's what we need to do.

BONNIE. I don't know about that Jean. I'm not much of a hippie type and besides I wouldn't know the first thing about buying dope.

JEAN. No, the part about burning their bras in the streets. Why don't we show our solidarity as women and burn our bras in the streets?

BONNIE. I think it's against the law.

DIANE. They're our bras, we should have the right to burn them. Right?

JEAN. Let's do it!

TRACY ANN. Yea!

JEAN. You've seen the cigarette ads that say "You've come a long way, baby?"

TRACY ANN. You bet.

JEAN. Well, have we?

TRACY ANN. *(Thinking about it.)* Uhhh.

JEAN. And if not, will we?

TRACY ANN. I don't know.

JEAN. Sure we will!

TRACY ANN. Sure we will!

JEAN. Well, I for one am tired of being tapioca.

TRACY ANN. Me too.

JEAN. I say we join in the movement.

TRACY ANN. Where do I sign up?

(JEAN starts to take off her bra under her dress.)

JEAN. There's no sign up, ya just gotta take off your bra.

TRACY ANN. *(Sudden panick.)* What?!

JEAN. C'mon girls, what do you we have to lose by burning our bras?

BONNIE. Support, for one

DIANE. Well, I'm tired of support.

(DIANE starts taking off her bra under her dress.)

SINCLAIR. Any chance to unleash the twins is fine by me.

(SINCLAIR starts to unhook her massive bra.)

TRACY ANN. *(She looks around confused by what is happening.)* Uh, Jean, about the...

JEAN. How about you Bonnie? Let's take a walk on the wild side.

BONNIE. I don't know about this...

TRACY ANN. *(Nervously raises her hand, shirting from foot to foot.)* Jean...*(JEAN waves her off.)*

BONNIE. What will the neighbors think?

JEAN. We are your neighbors.

BONNIE. Good point.

(BONNIE starts taking off her bra.)

TRACY ANN. Oh boy.

DIANE. How about you, Tracy Ann?

TRACY ANN. I can't.

JEAN. I'll buy you another one.

TRACY ANN. It's not that, I tried to tell you...I lied earlier.

BONNIE. About what?

TRACY ANN. When I told you that I wear a bra.

JEAN. And you don't?

TRACY ANN. I don't.

SINCLAIR. Isn't that a bite in the ass.

(DIANE and SINCLAIR pull their bras out of their dresses at the same time so that both bras are right next to each other. DIANE'S smaller satin bra is dwarfed by SINCLAIR'S massive, drab industrial machinery. All stare at the bras, shocked by their difference.)

JEAN. The beauty and the beast.
SINCLAIR. Ha-Ha-Ha...Very funny.
JEAN. Does anyone have a match?
BONNIE. You're not going to do it in here.
JEAN. No, we'll take it outside. Does anyone have a match?

(The ladies look in their pockets and purses.)

BONNIE. I think I have some matches somewhere in the kitchen.
JEAN. I'll help you look.

(JEAN and BONNIE EXIT.)

DIANE. Actually I think I have some matches somewhere in my...

(DIANE continues to sift through her purse. She dumps out the contents on the coffee table and finds a pack.)

DIANE. Ta da!
SINCLAIR. Great. Let's get this show on the road.

(Gathering up all the bras.)

    TRACY ANN. Shouldn't we wait for them?

    SINCLAIR. Tell you what, you stay here and tell them we're out front. Diane and I will get this bonfire in gear.

(Before DIANE and SINCLAIR head out the door SINCLAIR stops DIANE in her tracks.)

    SINCLAIR. *(Holds up the handful of bras.)* Well Diane, welcome to the neighborhood.

(DIANE and SINCLAIR EXIT out the front door. TRACY ANN watches from the window. JEAN and BONNIE ENTER.)

    BONNIE. See, I knew I had some kitchen matches somewhere. That stove pilot light is always going out. I keep telling Richard to fix it, but he's such a procrastinator.

    JEAN. Typical of men. *(Looking around the room.)* Where's Diane and Sinclair?

    TRACY ANN. They found some matches and now they're out front about to burn the bras.

    BONNIE. Out front?

    TRACY ANN. Yea, in the driveway.

    BONNIE. Maybe we should burn them on the patio instead...I mean...the driveway is so...*(Dawns on her.)* Oh my god, not the driveway! *(She rushes for the door.)*

    JEAN. What's wrong with the driveway?

    BONNIE. Because the driveway is covered with...

*(A huge blaze is heard going up outside the house. DIANE
screams. We see the orange glow of the flames through
the door and window.)*

BONNIE. *(Cont'd)* Gas!
JEAN. Get a fire extinguisher! Call the fire department.
BONNIE. Tracy Ann, Quick, there's an extinguisher in
the kitchen.

*(TRACY ANN EXITS through the kitchen door seconds later
bursts out dragging a fire extinguisher.)*

TRACY ANN. I'm coming Diane!

*(She runs across the stage out the front door. JEAN furiously
dials the rotary phone.)*

BONNIE. *(Yelling out the door.)* DROP AND ROLL, DI-
ANE! DROP AND ROLL!

*(We hear the sound of an extinguisher being released in short
bursts.)*

JEAN. *(Into the phone.)* Hello? Hello? Operator? Get me
the fire department.
BONNIE. *(Looks back outside, call to TRACY ANN.)*
That's right, Tracy Ann, keep rolling her around. Good girl.
JEAN. Yes, fire department, hello? We have a fire over
at 126 Sutcliff Road. What kinda fire? Well, it's a...uh...a bra
fire...

BONNIE. *(Yelling out the door.)* Tracy Ann, there's a flare up on Diane's shoe.

(More sounds of the off stage extinguisher short bursts.)

JEAN. *(Pause)* So what if we were burning our bras to show our solidarity, what's it to you? *(Pause)*

BONNIE. Good girl Tracy Ann.

JEAN. Excuse me, this is not a laughing matter!

BONNIE. *(To JEAN.)* It's ok, they put Diane out.

JEAN. *(Into the phone.)* Fine, buddy, we don't need your help anyway.

(She slams the phone down on the cradle.
SINCLAIR, and TRACY ANN slowly ENTER supporting a badly singed and dazed DIANE. DIANE'S clothes and hair are still smoking. Her lip is bleeding as well.)

BONNIE. Oh you poor dear, Are you all right?

TRACY ANN. Yea. I'm fine.

BONNIE. Not you, I meant Diane.

DIANE. I think so.

BONNIE. Sit her down on the couch. I'll get some towels.

DIANE. It all happened so fast. I threw the match on the pile of bras and whoosh all I saw was a flash. I didn't know those tricot cups were so flammable.

BONNIE. It wasn't the tricot cup, it was the gasoline in the driveway

DIANE. *(She feels the back of her head and winces.)* I think I have a bump on my head as well.

(BONNIE grabs some ice out of the ice bucket and wraps it in a towel.)

TRACY ANN. I think you hit your head when you dropped and rolled into that birdbath.

JEAN. Are you sure you're okay?

DIANE. Yes, I'm fine.

TRACY ANN. And I really liked that dress too.

DIANE. I got it on sale.

TRACY ANN. Where'd you get it?

JEAN. Could you cut the shopping talk. Diane just blew up on Bonnie's lawn.

DIANE. Did we burn the bras?

SINCLAIR. Ooooh yea.

DIANE. Then we've shown our solidarity.

BONNIE. Yes, we did.

JEAN. We did indeed. Let me get you some water.

TRACY ANN. Bonnie, before, I meant what I said. You are beautiful. I know it. I know that someday I'll be stretched out and sagging and my breasts will dangle like...what will they dangle like, Sinclair?

SINCLAIR. *(Casually)* Like a topless Zulu women in a National Geographic magazine.

TRACY ANN. Yes, it's so gross. I don't want that to happen, but it will. And when it does, I hope I look half as good as you.

BONNIE. *(Deeply touched.)* Thank you,

TRACY ANN. You're welcome.

BONNIE. That means a lot to me.

TRACY ANN. No problem.

BONNIE. Gimmie a hug.

(They cross to hug. JEAN starts to pour herself another scotch.)

SINCLAIR. Well, Diane, too bad you weren't turned around during the flare up.

DIANE. Why's that?

SINCLAIR. Maybe you could've burned off a couple pounds of that sad looking caboose.

DIANE. That's it!

(DIANE becomes fierce she grabs a throw pillow and attacks SINCLAIR. SINCLAIR retaliates with a pillow — all out war ensues.

RICHARD ENTERS to see his wife embracing TRACY ANN and giving her a kiss. He sees the pillowfight, and JEAN just pick up the whole bottle and take a drink.)

RICHARD. HEY! What the hell is going on here?

(They all stop in mid-action. Ladies all laugh BONNIE steps back and looks around at the situation.)

JEAN. *(Laughing harder, then...)* Oh god, I think I just peed.

BONNIE. *(Matter-of-factly.)* Well, Richard, I lied. When you're not around, we have liquored-up lesbian pillow fights.

RICHARD. You have...Fer Christ sakes, half the front lawn is gone, the Peterson's mailbox is in ashes and I found this pile of...of...what the hell is this?

(He holds up the still smoking pile of burned bras.)

JEAN. Well, girls, on that note, I think it's time we leave.

BONNIE. No, don't go.

JEAN. No, Bonnie, I think we'll finish up the liquored-up lesbian pillow fight at my place after we get Diane checked out at the emergency ward.

TRACY ANN. Yes Diane, we'll get you some Bactine and some gauze.

(All slowly walk past RICHARD while giving him an evil look. Each grab their bra. DIANE stops to shake RICHARD'S hand. Dumfounded, RICHARD shakes her hand.)

DIANE. Hi, I'm Diane Whettlaufer, you must be Dick. You have a beautiful house and a wonderful wife. I hope we can do this again sometime.

(SINCLAIR is the last to leave.)

SINCLAIR. Are you sure you don't want me to rip his balls off?

BONNIE. No, not today. Thanks anyway.

(As SINCLAIR walks past RICHARD she pretends to grab for his balls. He immediately covers them for protection.)

SINCLAIR. Watch it...Dick.

(All are gone leaving BONNIE and RICHARD standing in uncomfortable silence. BONNIE begins to straighten up the room.)

RICHARD. *(Angry)* I don't even want to know what I just saw!

BONNIE. *(Stifles him.)* There's nothing to explain.

RICHARD. Oh really!

BONNIE. Really!

RICHARD. *(Cowers back.)* Okay.

BONNIE. Why are you back so soon?

RICHARD. I, uh...felt...I was at the bowling alley, and well, I felt...I felt kinda bad about what I said to you.

BONNIE. Oh really?

RICHARD. It wasn't right. I shouldn't have said that.

BONNIE. No, you shouldn't have.

RICHARD. I know.

BONNIE. *(Starts to make herself a drink.)* You know, maybe we're not the same people we were twenty years ago.

RICHARD. No, we're not.

BONNIE. I'm not finished. And maybe we both don't look the same. I think we should stop for a moment and realize we are different.

RICHARD. Yes, we should.

BONNIE. That's how life works...It just hurt.

RICHARD. I'm sorry.

BONNIE. I'm not that same girl you married twenty years ago...I know it that...but I don't want to know it. I'm the woman who had your children. I'm the woman who took care of this house and most of all I'm the woman who took care of you.

RICHARD. I know.

BONNIE. Well you don't know enough! I need attention...and sometimes... not all the time...but sometimes I need to know you still think I'm attractive. Not to the world, but to you. I don't mind being invisible to other men. I just don't want to be invisible to you.

RICHARD. You're not.

BONNIE. Sometimes I just need to know that.

RICHARD. You're still attractive to me, Bonnie...Really.

BONNIE. *(Touched)* Thank you.

RICHARD. And I just wanted to say...

BONNIE. Why don't you just shut up before you ruin the moment.

RICHARD. Okay.

BONNIE. *(Straightens, serious.)* Now this is the program...no exceptions. We have one more year until Richie Junior leaves the house. You'll show me I'm valuable or I'm walking out a day later.

RICHARD. Wait, you're gonna leave me?

BONNIE. If I have to.

RICHARD. But...

BONNIE. No buts. Treat me good, pay attention and... and...I want sex!...regularly.

RICHARD. Regularly?

BONNIE. Regularly!

RICHARD. How often is regularly?

BONNIE. *(Chugs the rest of her drink.)* Starting now... let's go.

(BONNIE storms defiantly out of the room.)

BONNIE. *(O.S.)* Richard!
RICHARD. Yes, dear.

(Cowering, RICHARD follows. He passes the bar and pauses to take a bottle of liquor with him as he EXITS.)

FADE TO BLACK

COSTUME PLOT

Tracey Ann   yellow cigarette pants
                        white sleeveless sweater with pink, yellow
                        and turquoise stripe
                        pink poncho (remove on entrance)
                        nude body slimmer
                        tan huarache loafers
                        yellow plastic earrings, necklace and bracelet
                        yellow and white scarf tied around ponytail
                        wedding ring
                        green raffia purse
                        blonde ponytail

Sinclair   green paisley dress
                        pregnancy pad body suit
                        white bra
                        tan flats
                        lg shelled and sequined straw purse

*Bonnie, Jean, Diane and Sinclair remove their bras onstage

Bonnie   tan knit skirt with matching top
                        beige girdle and bra
                        beige pantyhose
                        brown loafers
                        tortoise shell and gold chain necklace and
                        matching earrings
                        gold watch
                        wedding ring
                        glasses on chain (worn during punch recipe

scene)
bright blue apron - removed on stage
lt auburn wig

Richard   brown polyester jeans
white tank undershirt
brown, orange and tan plaid camp shirt
black sneakers with grass stains
white socks
on stage change in scene 1
mustard bowling shirt
brown loafers
white jacket (carried, not worn)

Jean   purple and lavender jersey dress
matching coat/jacket (remove on entrance)
black girdle and black lace bra
taupe pantyhose
taupe pumps and envelope purse
purple iridescent brooch and earrings
silver and diamond watch
wedding ring and cocktail ring
black bouffant wig

Diane   ice green & cream polyester knit dress
matching suit jacket (remove in act 2)
white girdle and bra
cream pantyhose
lt green pumps and matching plastic box
purse
lt green neck scarf

lt green pearl button earrings
silver watch
cream pill box hat
blonde flip wig
after explosion change to
burned dress and scarf
distressed wig
black soot on face
dirt on knees

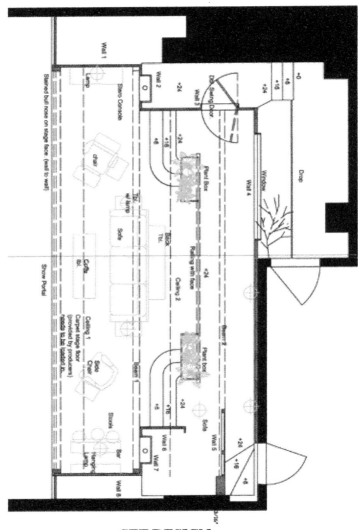

SET DESIGN

SIDE SPLITTING,
LAUGH 'TILL YOU CRY FARCES...

Tom, Dick and Harry
By Ray and Michael Cooney
What happens when two ne'er do well brothers decide to help their other brother and his wife adopt a baby? The answer involves two illegal immigrants, a truck full of smuggled goods, body parts from the local morgue and a night of hysterical mistaken identities and ingenious lies!

Never Kiss a Naughty Nanny
By Michael Parker
A real estate boss wants to sell a piece of property so badly, he pays his secretary and a salesman to pose as renters in order to entice a couple to purchase the house. But of course nothing is working right, all of the appliances seem to have a mind of their own, and even the maintenance man is in on the plot– he shows up dressed like a Nanny, and becomes too busy to fix anything while he tries to keep his cover and sell the house!

Leading Ladies
By Ken Ludwig
Two poor actors decide to play the ultimate roles when they hear a little old lady is about to die and leave her fortune to two nephews no one has ever seen. They decide it's the perfect gig for them, but when they arrive to collect their cash, it's only to find that the money was left to two long-lost *nieces*. But a little gender confusion won't deter these gents! Or rather, it won't deter these *"ladies."*